JAYCEE

A Heroine's Journey

ROBERT J. KOWALSKI

ISBN 978-1-64349-441-8 (paperback)
ISBN 978-1-64349-442-5 (digital)

Christian Faith Publishing, Inc.
832 Park Avenue
Meadville, PA 16335
www.christianfaithpublishing.com

Printed in the United States of America

Dedicated with love…

To all the strong women throughout the world, who have—for centuries—been relegated to a second place role in the churches of most organized religions.

You are our greatest and best hope in growing our compassion for each other and spreading the truth.

I would like to thank my mother, Elizabeth, for being her sweet self, Kristen Kowalski, who is the inspiration for Sister Kristen, my sisters Marylynn, Deb, and Michele. My Sister-in-law, Maryanne.

Thank You to my glorious Son, Jacob, for his support and my brother Jim Kowalski for all that I have learned from him. Thanks also to Brightstar and Wes Hamilton and Ron BEAR Cronick for their guidance along the way.

All strong and smart influences on my life.

With endless admiration and gratitude, Robert Kowalski.

Introduction

A woman, however learned and holy, may not take
it upon herself to teach in a assembly of Men
                    —The Synod of Carthage 398 A.D.

There are many paths to God and religion is just one of them. Imagine what the world would think or the questions that would be raised if Jesus lived now and was a woman teacher and prophet.

In my book, Jaycee explores that question.

The tale takes place in the small town of Serenity.

The issues and challenges Jaycee and her friends face are modern and connectable to us now.

I have often wondered why women are not allowed to be priests and are not celebrated in the Catholic Church to the degree that men are and have been for centuries.

I tell this very profound and complex tale in a lighthearted and hopefully thought-provoking way.

My goal is to fuel our collective goodness and to help awaken the churches toward gender balance.

Foreword
by God

Man can hardly even recognize the devils of his own creation.

—Albert Schweitzer

Why tell this story?

I get it; it's a valid question.

Throughout my time, which coincidentally is all time, I have been known by many names: Jehovah, Allah, Yahweh, but most of you simply know me as God.

I created the universe and all the planets, but earth turned out in such a perfect way that it is rare for me to have to investigate what has gone wrong. Or, more fittingly, what is about to go wrong and will ruin my creation. However, from time to time, it does happen. People are amazing, and believe me, I know amazing. Yet, it is certainly within them to destroy each other. Previous generations would say "bummer," the current one would say "sad."

Throughout time, I have given out trinkets of hope. Take for example a box I had delivered to a young and strikingly beautiful girl named Pandora. I know you've heard that story. A messenger of mine, dressed in rags, handed her the box and gave her one simple instruction:

"Never open the box."

"But, it is so beautiful, how can I not open it?"

"You can enjoy its beauty. But, if you open it—" He stopped short, remembering my instructions not to tell her what was in the box. "You should enjoy the beauty you see. Because the beauty you see is the true value."

ROBERT J. KOWALSKI

Surprisingly, Pandora did not open the box. She admired it, held it, and occasionally shook it to see what she could hear inside. Of course, she heard nothing. What lay within was silent and stealthy.

For many decades, she was wise and followed my messenger's warning not to open the box. But, in the end, her curiosity got the better of her. She could no longer withstand the pressure of waiting. So, in the dark of night, while the world around her slept, she walked to her table and lifted the box. For a longtime, she simply admired the box. She held it. She slid her fingers around the jewel-encrusted sides. And, before opening the box, she closed her eyes, not knowing what to expect.

She took a deep breath. Then she opened it.

Nothing more than what seemed like a puff of air escaped, and Pandora was confused. The box appeared empty. She sat it back down on the table, and walked away, disappointed.

Unlike the stories you have heard or read about Pandora's box, she was actually quite unaware of what she had unleashed with that mere puff of air. But all that is bad in the world had escaped. She released jealousy, hatred, fear, anger, betrayal, and violence to prey upon mankind. But, like most gifts, I pass on for humans to hold, I also included a glimmer of hope. The last thing to escape from the box was a fragrant scent of jasmine. Pandora smiled at the sweet aroma that suddenly filled her nostrils, not even realizing it was the final gift from the wretched box.

The scent of jasmine was the scent of hope, which with my unending grace, escaped along with all the evil.

There are times when I wonder if hope still exists. The crusades were not of my devising, yet they claimed to be in my name. The holocaust was also not mine, yet the embellishments I passed onto man, such as the Ark of the Covenant and my son's chalice (as simple as it was), were highly sought after. Perhaps, I would have allowed them to be found had so much evil not been in search of them. In the end, I pushed forth the water, and a steady stream of cloud cover to allow the allies access to a beach and a battle they could not have won without my help.

8

And so, it was a tense world. I had been pushing man forward for so many millennia, that even I was becoming tired. Then it was man's turn to surprise me. They began to fight evil . . . and win. I stepped back and have not had to intervene as the world appeared it would finally find peace and defend itself from evil.

Until I received a poem.

Yes, a poem. You may not understand the power of a mere poem, or for that matter, the power of a young woman. The poem I will share now, and more about the young woman, the author of the poem, in a moment. She was questioning her faith; in fact, she was questioning all faith.

> It was I who shot the arrow through your stained-
> glass window.
> I stood silently listening for the rattle of fletching
> as it chromed off your
>> frozen statue of three miracle myths.
> You could not see me in my wrap made of leather
> from the gifts of Earth.
> My bow would not fit in your collection plate,
> I fear,
>> My lawn exceeds the acquired length of
> one-quarter nap.
> I surely cannot contain my Gods in your taber-
> nacle trap.
> There is no need for me to confess my sins.
> In a darkened screened coffin to a silhouetted
> grin.
> It was I who stood on that hill and watched your
> procession of luxury cars,
> Vying for the coveted first row pew of religious
> stars.
> All straining to catch a glimpse of the next row's
> sins.
> Like cattle you respond to the bandleader's cue to
> rise, to kneel.

Breathlessly, you wait for that grand moment
when you can march in line,
Head solemnly bowed hoping to take a part of
God home with you this time.
It was I who watched and turned to the sky,
    An uncivilized savage,
    I began to cry.

She has faith in me, yet little faith in the men who claim to spread my word. It is the right of man to question. Yet, when those who invoke my word do not exemplify their meaning and intention, how does my flock not question them?

This gives me pause to take action. A simple poem. One of the most powerful weapons I have given to man.

As infrequently as I visit earth, I truly do enjoy it. My creation, if I say so myself, is quite enviable. As you can guess, if I were simply to come upon someone in human form and said, "Hail, for I am God," they would undoubtedly run away. Or maybe they would lunge at me with a sword, which of course would do nothing but irritate me. That's what I get for giving humans the ability to think. So, when I venture to earth, I choose the form I feel best fits my motive. Say for example, I must get someone's attention. I may arrive as, well, a burning bush. I hear that's a popular story.

I come in many shapes and forms, and when I really want to test the human race, I will simply whisper my words, which indeed must be whispered, for if I were to speak in a manner more befitting *The Almighty One*, you would be torn to shreds by the mere force of my words. In my whispers, words flow more gently (yet powerful) in a soft rhythmic and intoxicating beauty I call poetry. Are you now seeing the value I place on poetry? It has impact. Yes, poems are a reflection of me. They, like Homer's muses, hold man mystified and share with the spirit of man, not the mind, how I would like the world to change. Many have received my poetic messages. Perhaps, you recall the story of a rather lazy man named Noah who rose above criticism and shame to build a great ark. One that saved humanity. And, there was Moses and the burning bush. There have been many more such stories; all true. Some you have heard, but there are many you have not. Sometimes, it is a subtle change, which influences the most.

One might ask why I don't simply fix earth and correct its problems myself, instead of sending a messenger. There are a couple reasons: first, I gave humans the ability to resolve their own issues. I may drop a few helpful hints—breadcrumbs to follow, or help pave a path, but without defeating the evil Pandora let loose millennia ago, humans will never survive alone.

Secondly, if I were to fix the earth's problems, I would have to destroy it and start over. And I did that once already with the Great Flood. Of course, as questioning humans, you debate whether one of my most amazing events even took place. Well, yes, Noah did hear me, and he honestly exceeded my expectations. His animal gathering was quite a feat. Good man, that Noah. Opposed to what man will glorify, he was no doubt one of the laziest men I'd ever created, yet he turned into one of the hardest working. That was his own doing. I had nothing to do with it. He had a genuine fear of snakes, which he did a pretty good job working out for himself. Noah is one of the few who I like to say, did a decent job of putting the cover back on Pandora's box.

As you can see, if I am on Earth, it is because there is a problem. What most people don't realize is that it is the small things that make up the big picture. Like the tiniest pixels that make up the digital images you stare at all day. Even the smallest change can affect bigger changes ahead. For example, if you wake up five minutes late, you can either accidentally bump into your future spouse, or miss that same person, which leads you in a new direction in life. Take another poem, one of hope and change. One written by the same young woman who questioned my messengers. She wrote:

> Decades of togetherness are to time but a whisper
> in the winds.
> None of the time spent wasted, and surely none
> of that time a sin.
> When life's review is glimpsed

and we turn to look back on our path.
We will see that time spent with each other
was meant to be, but never meant to last.
Knowing this, we should hold each other gently
in our palms.
Bless the times we share and ignore any wrongs.
Lift our souls skyward, spread our wings once
again.
Sing our earthly human songs and let our hearts
begin to mend.

This young woman, Jaycee, is my next Noah. She is the symbol for change. Her humble and poetic nature will show you that it is not the question of faith people should concern themselves with, but rather the actions you pursue to find your faith.

What this young girl, Jaycee Woods, does not realize is that I have been with her for some time now. Watching for the moment she was ready. And that time has come, as it is now her turn to step away from the safety and protection of her shell, and change the world. Jaycee lives in the small town of Serenity, Minnesota. And that's not happenstance either.

Serenity is a quaint town where everything just seems too *right*. Where even the worst person, isn't *that* bad. Until, that is, the sleek black limousine with the Whalemart emblem on its doors slowly and quietly glides down Serenity's Main Street in three . . . two . . . one . . . *bump.*

I bet you didn't feel much there. But neither did Pandora when she opened her beautiful jewel-encrusted box. A puff of air back then; a glimpse of elegance now.

Then came the trouble, and again the very existence of every man, woman, and child on the planet is again at risk. Unless Jaycee can find it in her heart to listen closely to the small white squirrel lingering in a tree branch above her head.

The squirrel? Yes, that's me.

Why did I choose to inhabit the form of a squirrel? Well, they're cute, aren't they? Everyone loves squirrels even very bad people seem to soften in their presence. I've seen serial killers feeding gray squirrels in the park, sustaining their little furry lives, even while they contemplate taking human ones.

And I want to send the message that I am available to everyone, every day. I am right in your own backyard. I am in nature. These are not times that a lofty guy perched on a gilded throne, or a burning bush in the desert is the best choice. I want to be a more accessible and relatable God this visit. That is why I am here to help my newest messenger move herself along a bit.

I do need to figure out what to do with this acorn in my paws, and why I have such an insatiable urge to hide it. You see, even I'm prone to questioning my own rules and urges while on the planet. No one, after all, has authority over the Almighty—*even* the Almighty.

Perhaps, someday, you will talk of Jaycee the way you talk of my son's first visit.

I must say I am not sure how you lost the message of my last effort to show you how to live in this unique world I created for you. You were, and are, a very important and crucial part of the creation and concept of the world just by your mere thoughts. As you think, you manifest. However, more on that later.

But seriously, how did you lose sight of my wonderful son and squander his compassionate sacrifice? *Yes, it was his idea, I tried to talk him out of it, and did not think it would go well.* How did you toss aside his humble example of walking the countryside in sandals and a simple robe, telling childlike stories of how to live and be *in* this world but not *of* it? How did man turn that example of humility into the Vatican and the Catholic Church being the wealthiest single entity on the planet? Was Jesus not a man of modesty? Did he not live as a pauper when he could have a lived as a king? The Vatican is in many ways the recreation of Pandora's box. It glitters with wealth on the outside, but carries within it the vices of the world and only a smudge of hope. Man has appointed an infallible God on Earth, who speaks in my name. Man has taken free will and published it in his own making, ignoring the message my son tried hard to pass unto you.

Despite how man deciphered my son's message, I am proud of him. His impact was beyond anything I could have expected. Even to this day, man discusses at length his importance, and debates his message. But a young woman steps into the room of one of my messengers. A messenger who himself can learn a lot from a child. A young woman I happily call my lamb.

Just this morning she wrote another poem I am rather fond of. She ventures to test her own journey in life. Remarkable for such a young woman. Simply remarkable.

> No one gets everything.
> There is always a missing piece.
> The long road is ever traveled.
> The journey far from complete.
> There is a twinge of sadness.
> A glimpse of regret.
> Love that never ripened.
> Promises never kept.
> We all run out of time.
> Not able to complete.
> The woods are full of darkness.
> The meadow flowers smell so sweet.
> No one gets everything.
> That is a truth we will repeat.
> We all must bite the bitter fruit before we know
> the sweet.
> Dying is a form of life. Life is but the act of dying
> daily.
> Death the new beginning of being.
> Shadow edges light and light blinds the never
> seeing.
> Earth will keep on spinning and the next round
> of searching will
> begin.
> The endless pursuit of something.
> The tireless need to win.

Many have told the story of my son, Jesus, but much of it was told wrong, and it changed, not for the better, over several centuries. The stories were twisted by the storyteller to change what he thought was wrong, not what Jesus or myself tried to say. With such a motive, I'm sure you can understand how the Vatican came to be—an entity built on corruption and deriving wealth from the fear of the weak.

Admittedly, the church has improved of late. It struggles yet, and sometimes, it is the ramblings of a confused young woman with questions who changes one of my flock.

I will not allow man to tell another false story in the name of a messenger again. This is the story of that young poet, Jaycee. This is her story in her own words. The way a story should be told – from the words of my messengers. Not from the words of false prophets or twisted fable tellers.

I will watch and wait. In the meantime, I still need to figure out why I have an insatiable urge to hide nuts in the base of this tree, and why everyone keeps taking pictures of me. I'm just an ordinary squirrel, even if my coloring is a bit odd. I'm pure white you see, not sure why that happened. I'm not given to seeing color in my creatures, human or otherwise, and I wish humanity would be more like me in that regard. Color is, after all, merely an illusion of light and pigmentation reflecting Earth's magnificent palette. But oh, how you children got so lost in your bitter and divisive entanglements around skin color—fear-based misconceptions. It's distressing and disappointing to be sure.

Perhaps Jaycee can help them with that.

We are not human beings having a spiritual experience.
We are spiritual beings having a human experience.
—Pierre Teilhard de Chardin

Chapter 1

IN THE BEGINNING . . .

The beginning is the most important part of the work.
—Plato

When you drive at night and the rain begins to *rap tap tap* against your windshield, it brings a certain comfort, safety, almost a *womb-like* peace. The hypnotic *swishing* of the wiper blades, pushing away tears from the sky, and human exhaustion can account for many mysterious sightings. On this particular cold Minnesota night, it seemed like nothing could penetrate the veil of thick smog, and so when the brilliant flash of light burst in front of Joe's wet windshield, it caused him to swerve, hit the median, and blow out the front left tire. His warm, dry, safe cocoon—actually a well-used minivan—became a wreck in the *thump* of a heartbeat.

"What was that? Did you see that?"

"Yes, dear," the passenger said to the driver. "It blinded me too. And now we're in a mess."

Marilyn was pregnant and crazy close to her due date; about to give birth to their first child. Having planned with Joe to wait a few more years to have a child, it is a bit of mystery to her how she ended up pregnant. Well, she knew *how,* just not *exactly* how. As devout Catholics, they had used the old-fashioned "rhythm method" and had faith in it, but it seemed to have failed. She has been praying for easy labor and delivery, the kind that makes you wonder what all the fuss is about. When the light flashed in the sky, and Joe smashed the van into the median, her water broke.

"Uh-oh, Joe. Can you hurry up and change the tire?"

"Why, honey? Are you okay?"

"Yeah, but thanks to your awesome driving skills, we may be having a baby tonight." To punctuate the moment, she let out a loud groan. "Three weeks early."

Marilyn stretched out her legs and pushed her head against the seat. She began to pant like she'd learned in her birthing classes. During the time between her best friend's daughter's birth (her only experience with the birth process) and this pregnancy, doctors—most of them male, she noticed—had decided that babies should be born without the benefit of the drugs her friend had recommended. Women were now criticized if they opted for pharmaceutical assistance during childbirth. "Natural" was the way to go.

"Tell that to the garden hose birthing the bowling ball," she lamented to her doctor.

He had merely smiled indulgently at her. "Don't worry. We will keep you as comfortable as we can. You'll be fine."

"How many babies have you had, exactly?" she asked.

He smiled again and patted her on the shoulder. "This delivery will be my two-hundredth. Relax. You've got this, Mrs. Woods."

Joe changed the tire in record time in spite of rain pelting his back and rivulets of cold water dripping off his nose. He pulled back onto the road and then got off at the next rest stop. Marilyn was sweating in spite of the cold temperatures, but she was being a trouper in Joe's opinion; not that he had a lot of experience, but the documentary he had watched on child birth had given him an appreciation for the miracle of birth.

They were on their way home from a three-day outing to sing Christmas carols, a long-standing tradition that the young couple was reluctant to cancel, in spite of the impending birth of their baby. Four choir members were in the van with them—two sopranos, one alto, and one bass. The community in need of their Christmas carols had recently suffered a devastating fire that had burned down their little country chapel.

"How you doin', babe?" he asked, almost whispering.

She opened her left eye just a tad and glared at him. "About to push a bowling ball out of my swollen, tired, aching body. How do you think I'm doing?" Her snarl contrasted starkly with his reverent whisper.

Someone in the back—Marilyn thought it sounded like the alto—began a chorus of "Oh, Holy Night" and despite the soothing words of the hymn, she was agitated.

As her water broke she had felt a sense of peace come over her. "Now!" she said loudly, over the singing, "Joe, you're going to have to pull over somewhere. I'm not gonna make it to the hospital. This baby is in a hurry."

Joe sped up, risking the Minnesota black ice he knew was lurking on the pavement, and soon spotted a roadside rest area, empty on this rainy freezing night. Everyone in their right mind was in church or at home, doing their holiday traditions, trimming the tree, or drinking eggnog. Oh, what he wouldn't do for a bracing cup of hot cocoa right then. He was about to welcome his firstborn child. He didn't even know if it would be a boy or a girl; they had decided to not know the child's gender and he had painted the nursery bright yellow. A carpenter by trade, Joe had built custom Shaker-style cabinets across one end of the room, with a letdown desk for when the child got bigger and needed to do homework. It not only saved money, but was quite a beautiful piece of furniture.

"Worse come to worst," he had explained to his wife, "if we ever have to sell the house, it will add value for the resale."

Once he'd parked as close as possible to the building that housed restrooms and vending machines, he hurried everyone into the overhanging shelter that backed up to the woods and a small pond. He then gathered all the sleeping bags and the pillows from the back of the van and prepared the best he could for what was to be. The five of them made a cozy nest of sorts between the soda machine and the one offering candy and chips, which blocked the wind. The big bright red concessions provided bookends, and Joe figured it was cleaner than the rest rooms would be.

"Call 911," Marilyn said between contractions. She wasn't worried about herself, she knew she could handle anything, but she had been cautioned that firstborn babies often encountered problems exiting the virgin birth canal.

"I'm getting no bars," Joe said, exasperated and scared to death. The choir members chorused, "No bars!"

Marilyn, being of good health and constitution, took it all in almost as if the whole event was taking place around and outside of her person. She willingly, without complaint or question, laid down on the pillows, raised her knees to her chest, and pushed with all her might. It was over before the rest of the little group had time to look around. If they had torn their eyes from the sight of Marilyn, her beet-red face like a neon sign advertising her efforts, they would have seen animals peering out of the woods behind the rest stop building.

A deer, with her tiny doe stuck to her side, looked on with big brown eyes; she understood the moment, as all animals do. A rabbit with a clutch of pups twitched her pink nose beneath a canopy of laurel bushes and seemed to smile. And strangely enough, there was a snow-white squirrel looking down from the highest branch of a barren tree. He too seemed to be smiling. But no one noticed.

The baby was—as they all are—pure, new, and joyously crying out as she gasped for air. Yes, it was a girl, all pink and wrinkly, quickly wrapped in a blanket hastily pulled from the storage well of the van by the soprano. The world and all that is good and bad enveloped her. From one womb into another, she passed. It was then that they noticed the raccoon, then another, and a hawk flew overhead and landed in a nearby tree, and they heard the rustle of a deer. It seemed that all of the forest had come to see what all the fuss was about, but even more than that, each creature, including the frogs from the pond, stopped their croaking and stared into the makeshift shelter at the baby girl. For one brief moment, there was silence. Even from the highway, as if everyone knew something miraculous had just taken place.

Then someone realized, "I've got four bars!"

Emergency services were called, and a white EMS van pulled up, extracted a stretcher from the back, and rushed over to the group huddled between the vending machines.

"Where's the patient?" the stocky female EMT asked.

Joe pointed down at Marilyn, cuddling the tiny squalling infant on her chest. "Right here. My wife and daughter are right here."

He and the others stepped aside and allowed the EMTs to help Marilyn, still clutching the baby, onto the chrome gurney.

Joe joined his wife and child in the back of the EMS van, handing the keys to the alto with instructions to follow them to the hospital.

One EMT whispered to the other, "Weird that this is happening on Christmas Eve, right?"

The other answered, "Yeah. And did you see all those animals? Creeped me out."

He flipped on the sirens and lights, and the little family sped toward Serenity, Minnesota's small community hospital. It was outdated, poorly equipped, and in dire need of modern upgrades, but there never seemed to be enough money in the town's budget.

Chapter 2

SETTLING DOWN
AND SETTLING IN

Who you are is what you settle for, you know?
—Janis Joplin

Several years later, ten to be exact, Joe and the family had set-tled into their small tract home in Serenity, population one hundred thousand souls, and boasting a beautiful lake in its center complete with band shell, where most of the local lovers get married. There were swan boats that were always busy on Sunday summer after-noons and an eighteen-hole golf course that runs along the lake run by an old gentleman from Ireland named Shamus Sweeny. He still carried his thick Irish brogue, even though he has lived in Serenity for over thirty years. He fancied the ladies, and the kids enjoyed his tall tales of a lost Ireland, its leaping leprechauns, and magical four-leaf clovers. His son, Jude Sweeny, is the mayor of Serenity. In spite of the town's goodwill toward old man Sweeny, many felt that Jude is just another corrupt politician on the take and out for himself rather than the community. In spite of record tax collections, pot-holes aren't filled, sidewalks are cracked, and the animal shelter had to close, leaving strays to fend for themselves.

A retired nun from the Catholic Church in Minneapolis, Sister Kristen, decided to use her own savings, scrimped from years of sell-ing crocheted Christmas ornaments, to open her own animal shelter. She rented an empty space in the town's main shopping strip mall, and volunteers built fencing and enclosures out back. She frequently found kittens and puppies in cardboard boxes on her doorstep, but kind citizens also left anonymous donations in the form of bags of dog and cat food; sometimes even envelopes with cash.

Joe and Marilyn were good citizens; Joe runs Heartland Hardware, the only hardware store in town, and enjoys a position of prominence and respect. His store is the center "anchor" store in the same strip mall where Sister Kristen has her shelter. Joe never sells unnecessary items to his customers, preferring to give them advice on how to fix up their properties on a dime. Marilyn is a stay-at-home mom, raising their daughter, Jaycee, and running a tight ship. She is the disciplinarian in the family. Joe is a pushover when it comes to their child. Marilyn is a fan of biblical instruction such as "spare the rod and spoil the child."

Heartland Hardware is the anchor store right in the center of a strip mall in the center of town. The mall has a nail shop, the Kountry Kafe, famous for their meatloaf sandwiches, a free walk-in health clinic, TV repair shop (owned by town councilman, Bill Barbassette), and of course the animal shelter run by Sister Kristen. It was truly the heart and soul of the town and nearly everybody found reason to visit the mall at least once a day.

It was during the club championship held in August every year that Jaycee's gifts were first brought to the forefront. She was caddying for her father, Joe, who was the defending champion. Jaycee and Joe were on hole number seventeen, a drivable par four and often the pivotal hole in many matches. Joe had just driven the ball nearly 330 yards and left into a shallow pot bunker with an easy up and down possible for his birdie and a chance to close out the match. His opponent and the president of the local bank, Devlin Carless, was about to tee off when suddenly he grabbed his chest and fell to the ground. The seemingly healthy forty-year-old man started turning a shade a blue that was not a natural color for anything but a swallow. Jaycee, then having just turned eleven back in December, calmly walked over to Devlin, cradled his heaving head in her young but sturdy hands, while she seemed to go into a momentary trance. It was just moments later that Devlin coughed and jumped to his feet, asking what had happened.

To tell the truth, no one really knew, not even Jaycee. She just did things that her heart told her to do and always had nothing but the best intentions in her actions. Joe always knew she was special, not because of the love he felt for her and her mother, but the way the birds seemed to follow her when she was in the woods and the butterflies would land on her when she rocked on the porch swing. It was little things—the whole world seemed to circle her and she seemed to notice and have time and a kind word for all from the elderly to the children in daycare she would make laugh with her funny faces. She never forgot a name. That alone was a miracle in itself. To care more for the people and the small things around you than yourself was just something she had always done, and it just seemed to flow from her spirit.

Chapter 3

A very small degree of hope is sufficient to cause the birth of love.
—Stendhal

Jaycee and Maggie were best friends; Maggie just lived life a bit louder. Jaycee thought of Maggie as someone with the volume turned way up. She had a tattoo on her lower back depicting two angels holding on to a vine of grapes. She had seen the picture somewhere in a book on Renaissance artists and it spoke to her of another time and a softer world. No one really saw Maggie for the loving and brilliant being she was except for Jaycee, who loved her deeply and always knew she was more then she let the world see.

It was in the girls' sixteenth year, and Maggie had fallen heart over head in love with a kindred wild spirit. His name was Joshua, and he was older by two years, from deep local Minnesota farming roots, and had that rare combination of sensitivity and strength not often found in a boy that age. He also had a bad boy wild side that Maggie adored.

She felt safe with him, and he let her into his world of poetry and art that he hid from the others. The story has been told throughout the world's history—two young souls finding comfort, and a haven in an all too often harsh and lonely world, at least seen through the eyes of teenagers.

Jaycee, sensing her dear friend's internal struggle, stayed up until dawn, hiding in her walk-in closet under a blanket "tent," helping her dear friend work through all the emotions, guilt, excitement, fear, and joy that is attached to milestones in a young girl's life. The greatest gift anyone can give another spirit is non-judgment and unconditional support to a fellow traveler who feels lost or off their personal path. Jaycee never criticized in these moments, but merely imparted her wisdom and sage advice, simply and clearly. She believed that we are all here to learn and grow and experience this wondrous earth; however, it was also important to be aware of a larger purpose and a grander plan.

She called it the Star World and mentioned that was the place her spirit parents and family lived. She would share this with all who asked but most passersby would laugh and wink, really not sure how to take this strange and beautiful creature called Jaycee. She called this place Star World because it represented a place that was larger than Mother Earth, surrounded by love and comfort, and there was room for many souls who wanted to do the good work to be received into the peace and tranquility it offered. The Native Americans called it *Walking the Sacred Red Path,* and she always liked that description because their traditions taught that all things are sacred and all people one, and they loved the gifts the world offered from the smallest bird to the great bears. She believed there were many names for living a life of integrity, gentle discipline, and unselfishness and that was one name, heaven was another, nirvana yet another, so the list was long and represented all corners of the earth, but their messages of goodness were very similar. For her, it was the Star World, and she had felt attached to that world from as long as she could remember.

Maggie was a passionate person and had a wonderment for life that most don't allow themselves to feel. She was good at everything she did, from sports to art, and she loved music; however, she felt that she really wasn't that gifted and struggled with her concept of self. She came from a wealthy background of what she called "stuff." But unconditional love was scarce in her household, and when her parents divorced, it threw her whole concept of what was created by Madison Avenue marketing of the perfect mate and life out the window. She felt like she was sailing alone with very few glimpses of the shore. Her mother loved her, but she withdrew into her own world of isolation and food to escape the pain that had enveloped her when her husband of twenty years left her to "go find himself," as he had put it. Maggie loved her father, but sadly, her father only loved himself. The hole was vast that he left, and like most wounds we incur on this planet, it was too deep to fill with anything the earth offers.

That is where Jaycee came in for Maggie. She had a strong sense of peace about her and contentment that came from some other place and that always intrigued and called out to Maggie. "How can I be more like you?" she would ask Jaycee.

The answer was the same.

"You are so beautiful to me, Maggie, and you are perfect in every way. I ask only that you love yourself and others the best you can, and give everyone the benefit of the doubt and a second chance, even the ones who hurt you the most."

And so the strong bond between the teenage girls, as unlikely and mismatched as it was, was about to be tested in ways neither of them had ever imagined.

Chapter 4

QUESTIONS, QUESTIONS, AND MORE QUESTIONS.

Going to church doesn't make you any more a Christian
than going to the garage makes you a car.
—Laurence J. Peter

Maggie walked with me as I headed toward Father Paul's office, which was situated in a wing of the church chancery, where he lived and worked. The big, beautiful stone cathedral has always been the anchor and centerpiece of Serenity. It is the scene of marriages, birth consecrations, and sadly, many funerals. Most of the town's citizens tithe even when they can't afford it. It is truly hallowed ground. The church members work hard to maintain the church grounds. There is a smaller Baptist church, and even a tiny Methodist chapel on the outskirts of town, but no observer would doubt the vast importance of the Catholic Church in Serenity.

It was the middle of my senior year, and it felt like my life was getting more and more confusing. Aren't things supposed to get clearer as you get older? I have more questions now than I did back when I used to caddy for my dad and help him win golf tournaments. Reading greens and judging club distances was a snap compared to being a teenager. Maggie is a constant source of worry for me.

"Damn, girl! Father Paul knows how to live. I should be a priest," she said, whispering close to my ear, her eyes sweeping the opulence of our parish priest's office.

Lavish velvet drapes in rich green, tapestries on the back wall, gold tassels, also left no doubt as to the value the church placed on its cleric. The priest was a man of worth and importance.

His massive quarter-sawn oak desk squatted solidly in the center of the room. Handcrafted as a tribute to the Hanging Gardens of Babylon, one of the seven ancient wonders of the world, it was a testament of an amazing carpenter. The twists of flowers and vines seemed to grow from the desktop, and delicately hidden within the tangled vines were cherubs, soft, and at least appearance-wise, plush. The desk was stained a deep mahogany, so rich that it seemed the tree rings, easily visible, had grown that color.

I recall Father Paul telling me he'd had the desk commissioned specifically for this office five years ago. Although he never revealed the cost to me, I assume it was more than some people's yearly salary. It looks to me like he believed the bigger the desk, the more important the person using it; but of course, I never said that.

Along the walls of Father Paul's office were a variety of hangings, from an original Rembrandt he said he'd received as a gift from Bishop O'Reilly for his service, to a framed mint condition, 1909 T-206 tobacco baseball card series. Heaven only knows what they are worth. He has several award plaques on another wall, and his credentials are posted behind his desk between two giant ferns. His jewel-encrusted pen collection filled two lighted glass cases, and his collection of shipwreck coins and artifacts took up two more. If you were a history buff, your jaw would drop at such marvels. For his small collection, Father Paul chose quality over quantity and took as much care in presenting his collections as he did in building them. Each protective glass case hooked to a security system that he never told me too much about, although with the number of tiny blinking red lights, I would bet laser sensors were involved, as well as touch sensors which he did tell me existed. Also, the door and windows into his office were all under security monitoring. He'd also hinted at other, more modern security traps for any would-be thieves. Maybe motion detectors.

I don't think he'd been carefully warning me; he is rather fond of me and I of him. More so, I think he wanted me to spread the word. Teenagers are notorious for pranks and quick money schemes. As the parish priest, Father Paul is an informal counselor when a student needs discreet emotional support, which I'm sure he is often used for.

"You sure you don't want to stay?"

Maggie tore her eyes from the Rembrandt and looked at me. She nearly scoffed at my question as she turned away, readjusting a lumpy backpack on her shoulders. "Nah, I got more important things to do than talk to a priest on our day off from practice."

"More important than hanging out with me?" I joked, knowing that she was going to go make out with her new boyfriend. Probably scrunched behind the bleachers, of all places. How cliché! But, that was Maggie, the quintessential cliché of a high school student. Always trying to "push the boundaries" and be as bad as she thought she could get away with.

Her text alert chirped. "Hold on a sec."

She glanced at the screen and giggled. Nearly blushed. Then tapped the screen a few times. "I have to go, Jaycee. You have a good . . . um . . . you have a good talk. Whatever it is you guys talk about."

"All right, cool. I'll catch you later. Behave, Mags."

"You know it. Hey, tomorrow morning. Let's go get ice cream."

"How about we volunteer at the animal shelter? You promised."

"Okay, yeah. Ice cream it is. I'll get Moose Trax flavor if that makes you happy."

Then she giggled and was out the door and down the hall, turning the corner and disappearing from sight before I could argue. That was Maggie. Glued to her phone, enamored of her boyfriend du jour, and gone before you had time to question anything about what she wanted to do, was going to do, or worse, had done. And she was my best friend, running on over ten years, and I was used to her weird ways.

The toilet from Father Paul's private bathroom flushed, the rude sounds of gurgling water startling me. I suddenly felt like I'd been intruding or plotting a heist of his valuable collections. Guilt made my face go all flushed and probably red, although there was no mirror and I couldn't see that. *Should I run? What if he thinks I'm nosy?* Then I heard water running and him tugging at a few paper towels before the door opened. I'd always wondered what his bathroom looked like. Was the toilet etched in gold? Like a real throne? Was the mirror made of such perfectly polished silver that your reflection was as good as a glass mirror? Did he have the likes of Picasso behind cases sunk into the wall for his viewing during contemplative pooping moments? They were all silly notions, I know, but Father Paul was a man who enjoyed the finer things in life, and everyone knows it. If you were from Mars and didn't already know that, the lavish rings he wore on nearly every finger would tell you.

"Oh! Jaycee. How are you? Come on in. I wasn't expecting you today."

He tossed a wad of paper towels into the trashcan by the door and composed himself. For the world, he looked like I'd just caught him doing something wrong, but everyone goes to the bathroom. I wanted to say, *Lighten up, Father.*

"Sorry," I said.

Usually, I did give him a bit of warning before I came by as our discussions often lasted a couple of hours. *Discussions!* I have to laugh at the word. They were more like heated debates. I have so many questions, and Father Paul is the only person I know who has travelled outside of our small town of Serenity. In fact, he's travelled around the world, like several times. In addition to the collections he has around his office, he also has photographs of his travels to China, Brazil, Ecuador, France, Italy, Nigeria, South Africa, and dozens of other places I'm sure I am forgetting.

His travels were actually a topic of one of our "discussions" one day. I couldn't understand how a priest could travel so much, or even why they would. Of course, I hadn't thought about one important role of the Catholic Church—missionary work. Father Paul had apparently served as a missionary for years. Although he did take time to point out that most of his work was done on his knees, in mud, helping to rebuild towns destroyed by natural disasters. This helped him learn about the culture and the people and adjust his sermons to what affected them most. He said his formal preaching was relegated to Sundays, unless someone wanted to talk about their faith. It never did take long for a small congregation to start up and then grow.

I admired Father Paul for his interest in helping people like that. Maybe he deserves all the beautiful artwork and collections in his office.

"I didn't really have a plan," I explained. "It's just that we don't have practice today, and I thought I'd stop by to say hello."

My sweetest smile punctuated the sentence. Hey, a girl has to work it, you know?

"Oh! Yes, I forgot. The Winds are heading to the state tournament, aren't you? I'm so proud of all of you. You know we haven't had a winning soccer program in . . . well, in as long as I can remember."

I couldn't help but tilt my chin down to hide my blush. It is no secret that the Winds had almost been the most laughable soccer team for decades. It wasn't until a couple years ago that we started winning, or at least not being a pushover team who chalked up wins for other teams. This year, everything just seemed to click, and we are not only winning, but winning a lot.

"We're all very excited. I'm a pretty good loser, Father, but winning is much more fun. Is that bad?"

He laughed. "No, it's not bad to enjoy winning. It is only bad if someone else's losing makes you happy. So, I bet you are happy with your team. Speaking of which, I hear that the Winds are underdogs going into the tournament, but under the table, they are favored to win. If I was a betting man, I'd say the Winds were a good bet to take it all, and make someone some good money on the side."

He gave me a big, theatrical stage wink and looked heavenward.

We all know Father Paul likes to gamble. It is no secret, even though he likes to pretend it is just between him and me. I think he told me one time that it is his escape. It is his one vice he's never been able to break. That was his description before he went on about how the devil has a hold on all of us. It is our job, he always says, to use the strength of our faith to break from those vices. Such as he has to break from his vice of gambling, I have to break from my vice of holding back my internal feelings with others. It sounded strange to me that that is a vice, but the more I thought of it, I wondered how it could not be one. I loved that talk.

"Well, come on then and sit down. I know you didn't just come here to say hi. Jaycee Woods is too much of a thinker. Like Da Vinci, you can't help but think and contemplate everything around you."

He walked around his desk and pulled the chair out a little for me to sit down then motioned me to join him at his desk. He went around to the other side, pulled out his chair, sat down, and propped his chin up with both hands as he looked at me the way a five-year-old kid would look up to his dad. With excited anticipation of what was to come.

I sat down, sliding my bag along the backside of the chair. "I don't know if I have a specific topic," I sighed.

Truthfully, there is a topic I'd been wanting to talk to him about for a long time. I just didn't know how to bring it up without hurting his feelings, or upsetting him.

He sat back in his chair. "Well, when you're ready, we can talk about it. I think you know what you want to say but are afraid to say it. I would like to remind you that everything you say to me is in complete confidence. I will not go to your parents, your friends, or anyone else at the school."

"I know, Father Paul," I said, biting my upper lip.

If he'd only known that what I wanted to talk about was him, maybe he would think twice about saying that. He didn't have to go to anyone else—only himself. I stopped myself from getting caught in a lapse and quickly sat forward. "And I appreciate that! I'm just not concerned about it."

"Well then, what is bothering you. I know you won't tell anyone else. It's difficult to keep things in." He jacked an eyebrow up and said, "Which I know you are prone to do."

"Yes, I know."

I wanted to hide it so much. I don't know what my problem is. I can't talk to most people about anything, and the ones I can talk to I can't seem to hold my tongue. "I just don't understand things," I blurted out.

"Good." He leaned forward, his eyes kindly fixed on me. "That's a start. What is it that you don't understand?"

"There are all these things the Bible says I should be doing. Things you say I should be doing. Be kind, help my neighbor, be faithful to God, and . . ."

"True. Those are things we should all be doing."

Then he paused to smile. That was the smile that often led to our biggest debates. The smile that realized there was much more to what I wanted to say.

"And, what is that final thing you were going to say?"

I let out a breath I'd been holding in too long. It came out like a frustrated sigh, but I wasn't frustrated, I just didn't know how to say what I wanted to say.

"Just let it out, Jaycee. I'm a big boy. I can handle it."

"Well, I sometimes wonder about Jesus. He was born in a manger surrounded by animals. Then as an adult he walked the Earth in sandals. I never remember hearing about a . . . what's the word? He never had an . . . entourage. A posse, like rappers and popstars do now. But he was a rock star in his time, right? I don't remember hearing about him having a tent, or living in a palace, or even having anything of his own. How could that be?"

"That's true. By all accounts, Jesus was a poor man."

"But he was the son of God? He was a king. The greatest king!"

"Those are all things you could say about him. He was also a humble carpenter. And jokingly not a very good one if he decided to be the son of God and take all our sins on his back. Seems to me a carpenter would have been a much safer, and stress-free choice for an occupation. Yet he did it."

"Well, what I'm getting at is that he was so poor."

"In possessions only. But wealthy in many other regards."

I put aside his comment in my mind, looking to what I wanted to say, slowly putting it all together. Father Paul continued to talk. I imagine he was talking about Jesus acting as Apollo in many ways, holding up the Earth for everyone else. He carried us on his back, so we had an opportunity to save ourselves from our sins. He saved us.

Then it came out, bursting from my mouth like a flood through a cracked dam. "Father, I don't understand how Jesus lived in poverty, preached modesty, and yet the church finds it okay to live in opulence. I've seen the Vatican and heard of its immense wealth. I've seen and heard of vast collections worth hundreds of millions of dollars. I just don't get it. Why should the flock live in poverty, while the church lives on a silver cloud?"

I wanted to take it back as quickly as it came out. It took everything in my power to not look around at Father Paul's own collection of wealth. Judging by his face, I could tell I didn't have to look around to get my point across. He heard it loud and clear. He looked like I'd slapped him in the face. I was horrified at what I'd said.

"I see."

He leaned back in his chair, and for the first time, I found Father Paul with no rebuttal or immediate comment on what I had to say. He glanced around his office as if he were trying to avoid my eyes.

I stood up, ready to run. "I'm so sorry, Father. I didn't mean to upset or attack you. I have just been thinking about this for a long time, and I don't know how to understand it. I'm sure there is a good reason. I'm sure I am just a dumb kid and don't understand. I just . . . I don't get it, and I—."

He held up a hand and motioned for me to sit back down. "You're right, Jaycee. Don't apologize."

I clamped my mouth shut and sat down, but just on the edge of the chair. I didn't expect that. Father Paul always had something to say that made sense. He always had a way of reassuring me that the church's intentions were good, despite my lack of understanding.

"I looked around the room, making sure he knew I meant the wealth surrounding me in an otherwise common office space. "Then I don't understand what all of this is."

He smiled, leaned his head to the side, and then rolled it as if he were stretching. He kind of looked like a kid caught with his hand in the cookie jar. "Well, this is me. I am human. I'm not going to sit here and tell you that the shepherd leads his flock from a stall in the same manger where the sheep sleep. I also won't tell you that all of the money the church has is for good, nor is it all for bad."

"Then, what is it for?"

He fidgeted, obviously a little more nervous than he thought he'd be when he first saw me in the doorway.

"Well, a lot of the money the church takes in—ours and others—is meant to help others. It takes money to help others. Some of it is an investment for the future, with the same intended purpose. And some of it . . ."

I waited, ready to bolt, but the words "get out of my office" never thundered from his mouth. There was no admission of guilt, no explanation of the wealth in his office, and even more so as you step along the hierarchy of the church. Rather, there was silence. For a long time, he gazed out the window between his collection of jeweled pens and shipwreck artifacts. He stared off as if contemplating his own future.

I fidgeted in the chair uncomfortably, wondering if he wanted me to leave, or if he was thinking of something to say. It would have been rude for me to just get up and leave. I felt as if I was surrounded by dozens of sleeping babies and my only way out was by walking on a creaking wood floor. Do I stay and wait, or do I go and risk waking the babies? I stayed put.

Ten minutes ticked by in total silence. It was like a battle of wills. Who would break first? Then something happened, almost as if an act of God himself to break the unbearable tension.

I jumped up and screamed, "Father, you're bleeding!"

Chapter 5

Autism is part of who I am.

—Temple Grandin

"Father! Your nose. It's bleeding."

Father Paul awoke from his trance. He smiled at me, back to his normal self, then reached for one of the desk drawers, pulled it open, and grabbed a box of tissues. He wiped the blood from under his nostrils, leaving a light smear of red above his upper lip. The spell was broken in dramatic fashion.

"Oh, don't worry, Jaycee. It's not a big deal. It's kind of a family thing. You know, winter equals dry skin, cracked lips, and bleeding nose."

He attempted a feeble smile and dapped at his nose with the bloody tissue. He didn't seem as convinced with his response as he wanted me to feel. His hands were shaking, and his face had taken on a ghostly pallor. It was scary.

"Are you sure you're okay? I mean, did I do something? Is this my fault? I didn't mean to offend you or anything I just—"

With the same distinct hand gesture he always used, that was devoted to strength and could stop a bus in its tracks, Father Paul again raised his hand and I went silent.

"Jaycee, shush now, child. You didn't offend me. You simply gave me something to think about. I should be the one apologizing. I should have not had you sit there for so long as I contemplated how to respond to you."

He took the bloody tissue from his nose, pulled out a Ziploc bag that had other bloody tissues in it, put his fresh one in the bag, closed it, and put it back in the drawer.

"See? Family trait. Happens all the time. Not your fault." Then he added, as if reading my mind, "And not a sign from God."

He was right, and in a strange way, revealing the small bag of bloody tissues made me feel as if he'd been honest with everything he was saying. It rebuilt a confidence in him I'd felt waning. He was still Father Paul, one of the good guys.

"I'm still sorry. I didn't mean to accuse you of anything. I am just curious."

He smiled at me as he replaced another tissue. "You didn't offend me, Jaycee. You are curious. It is your nature. Because you don't understand something doesn't mean it is wrong." He also added, "It also doesn't mean it is right. However, I don't want to mislead you into thinking what you see around you is wrong."

"I don't understand. These are collections. Aren't they? And very valuable?"

"Oh, sure they are. These are great collections. Yet, they are also investments. You know what stocks are, and probably mutual funds, after your economics class. But have you heard of tangible assets?"

I shook my head no, not knowing what Father Paul was getting at.

"Well, you mentioned the visible wealth the church has, right?"

I nodded.

"What if I were to tell you that when I assembled those base-ball cards, it cost me $10,000. But now, as a set, they are worth over $40,000. Those shipwreck artifacts are in an original state. They cost $75,000 to assemble. But, as people turn them into jewelry, or melt them down, lose, or destroy them, the value of mine grows, and they are now worth over $100,000. Those items are merely investments into the Serenity Parrish. They are investments into the town, our church, and, well . . . you. Life is not always happy. Natural disasters occur, the economy changes, people lose jobs. The fact is, that finer tangible assets do not fluctuate with those problems the way stocks do. So the church will often invest in high-end items to keep the value of money growing, while not fluctuating. Because you need it most, when most don't have it."

I stared at him, taking in what he was saying, but not know-ing how much of it I believed. It made sense, of course. Father Paul always made sense. But, there was something I couldn't wrap my head around. I just couldn't figure out what that was. Yet. But I knew I would.

"Do you understand, Jaycee?"

I nodded. "Yeah, I think so, Father. Maybe." Hedging my own bet. Trying to be honest.

He smiled and stood up. He walked around his desk and placed his hand on my shoulder. "I love our discussions, Jaycee. I'd like to continue this one, but I have more business to attend to. Maybe if you stop by next week we can continue."

The softness in his voice reflected doubt that we'd ever broach the subject again. This was the first, and last, time I would ever venture to ask why Father Paul's office was filled with valuables. I still trusted him, and I loved him as much as any of my friends, but I felt Father Paul may have had another vice . . . an addiction . . . more vicious than gambling.

"Thank you," I said, and stood up. "I really appreciate your time. I always come in here feeling empty, and leave feeling full."

The little bit of praise put a wide smile on his face as if I'd just handed a toddler a bucket of candy. I still had a big important question to ask him, but that could wait.

Johnny was waiting for me as I walked out of the priest's office. I couldn't believe I had been inside for almost an hour, although, admittedly, it was one of the shorter conversations between Father Paul and me. I laughed as I walked out.

"I did not want you to walk home alone, Jaycee," Johnny said to me, his guttural, deep voice stagnant and even as always.

I smiled at him, winking, "Thanks, Johnny. You're so sweet."

"What's the wink for?"

"I was just being silly. You know me."

"Of course, I know you, Jaycee. I have known you for . . ." He paused, glanced up to the flag flapping some twenty feet above us, as he calculated something in his head. "One thousand, seven hundred, and fifteen days, and seven hours." He chuckled then added, "And seven hours."

Whoever said Johnny was stupid, or worse, retarded, had another thing coming to them. Johnny is one of the nicest and most intelligent people I know. He is also my closest confidant. I can tell him anything and know it is locked under tight guard with no chance of ever getting out.

"I love when you do that. I wish I was as good at math as you are."

"I wish you were as good at math as I am too, Jaycee."

"Come on. Let's head home."

We walked along the sidewalk that bordered the outer edges of the school. It was getting chilly in late fall, but today is rather warm. Warm enough to not need a jacket yet.

"It is supposed to be 49.6 degrees today. The almanac told me, Jaycee."

"I know it's supposed to be colder, but you can't always rely on past information. Some years, it is cold. Some years, it is hot."

He didn't seem to ponder my comment, as usual. It was one of the cute curiosities of Johnny I adored. We crossed the street onto Elm Avenue.

"What did you and Father Paul talk about today, Jaycee?"

"Nothing much," I fudged the truth a little, but I didn't know how to tell Johnny about my question and how Father Paul answered it without Johnny starting Armageddon with his research into the church's wealth. If Johnny was anything, he was viciously devoted to research when he was curious about something. He would go as far as not sleeping for days while he went online. I like to call it boxing, otherwise sitting behind a box computer, despite the fact that he uses a laptop. Although, he was always quick to correct me that his laptop was in no way a box-type computer. "We just talked about Jesus living in poverty."

"Jesus was a man, Jaycee. He was not God. Why do they say he was God, Jaycee?"

"I don't know. Maybe I will ask Father Paul next time," I replied, although I am pretty sure any answer I would be able to give Johnny wouldn't be worthy of his question.

His questions have a way of sounding simple, but they're usually pretty deep.

"My dad said my grandma cannot live with us. I love my grandma, Jaycee."

"Why can't she?"

I didn't think money was the issue. Johnny's father is Mr. Carless, the president of the Bank of Serenity, and from what I've heard my parents saying, they're pretty well off.

"Mom wants Grandma to live with us. She is old and sick. I don't think my dad likes my grandma, Jaycee."

"I'm sure he does. There has to be another reason than he just doesn't like her."

"My mom and dad yell about Grandma at night. They think I am sleeping. I am not sleeping. My dad said it is not his job to watch Grandma. She needs to live somewhere else, Jaycee."

I think if I heard that about any other family I wouldn't have been surprised, but to hear Johnny's parents were arguing, especially about caring for a relative, was shocking. His family is very prominent in the church and present a caring and devoted family image. They seem like my own family. I didn't know what to tell Johnny. There was a gripping pain in my stomach at the thought that Johnny was sad. I would never know. As long as I'd known him, he'd never shown emotion. He may as well have been Spock from the TV series, *Star Trek*—same jet-black hair, same narrow and pointy face, and same matter-of-fact expression and manner of speaking. Had I not known any better, I would have thought Johnny was the younger Spock.

"I'm sure everything will be okay, Johnny. Your parents will work it out."

He didn't respond until we got to his home, two doors down from mine.

"Maybe Grandma can live in my room with me. It is big enough for two beds. Then Dad won't be as upset with Mom, and Grandma will not have to live somewhere else, Jaycee."

I could never tell if Johnny was looking for a response, or if he was merely stating what was on his mind. I knew it wouldn't work.

If his dad didn't want her there, it was for a reason. Although, I still couldn't fathom why such a good-natured family would ever argue over a beloved relative staying with them.

"I will tell my parents today when they get home from work. They will like my idea, Jaycee."

I bit my lip, not sure how it would turn out. "I'm sure they will, Johnny. You have a good night. I'll see you tomorrow."

I hugged him, and he walked away, and as usual, he just let his arms hang down at his sides, allowing me to hug him for my benefit, not his.

As I watched, Johnny opened the front door of his home, and disappeared inside.

I never knew if I should feel sorry for Johnny, or if he feels sorry for me. The world seemed so easy for him. Everything was black and white, but in my world, it seemed only gray.

I felt a small vibration in my pocket. I use my outdated, or as Maggie refers to it, my "dinosaur phone," so rarely I forgot it was even there. I pulled it out and flipped the top up. The message was from Maggie herself, in large block letters. I'd never been able to figure out how to change the font: NEED TO TALK!

Uh-oh.

Chapter 6

My best friend and I love to make fish faces.

—Beverley Mitchell

Maggie is my best friend and just happens to also be the prettiest girl in school. At least I've always thought so. After seeing her dramatic text, I promised to meet her somewhere private, and as I sat down on a fallen log overlooking our little village, I wondered how long it would take her to actually show up. She had seemed in a rush but refused to tell me what was going on. With Maggie, it could be anything. She did not prioritize well, and a bad hair day could be just as much an emergency to her as a meteor about to crash into Earth. Some people—mainly her parents and our teachers—were often irritated by this trait. I found it endearing. She kept me in constant bewilderment.

I pulled ear buds from my pocket, and within seconds, I was listening to the chaos of my classical playlist and mentally pictured myself seated in an audience two centuries ago listening to Mozart. I closed my eyes and could feel a smile tugging at the corners of my mouth. I know it sounds weird, but my mind has the ability to do that; it just takes me places like I'm really there. Make of it what you will.

The sun's rays touched my skin, almost summery but still comfortable. As much as I tried to put it behind me, and even while a young Mozart pounded the piano keys, I couldn't get rid of the thought of Johnny's parents arguing about his grandmother staying with them. Maybe Johnny just didn't know the whole story, or was confused by what they'd said. I mean, Johnny is a little . . . I don't actually know what I would call him. A savant maybe? An eccentric?

He isn't slow, although that's a common way to say it. He is probably smarter than anyone I know. Ultimately, he is either well aware of his parents' problems, or he is confused. Either way, he told me exactly what he thought was the truth. If I could depend on Johnny for anything, it would be that. More than anyone I know, including Maggie and my parents, I trust Johnny to always tell me the truth. At least the truth *as he sees it.*

My antique flip phone tells me it's been forty-five minutes since Maggie said she needed to talk to me. *Urgently.* I wish I could say I'm worried about her, but since she's notoriously late, I don't think there is a problem. Maggie runs on her own time.

As I wait, I find myself thinking about our other friends and how loyal they are. It is truly a blessing, and I always give a prayer of thanks for them.

Letty, for example, is a pixie of a girl with short spikey hair she colors purple. It makes her look punk, but she's the sweetest little thing. I think the nose ring is her way of showing disrespect for authority. She swears when she is an adult, she won't pay any taxes. Can't wait to see how that works out for her.

The opposite end of the spectrum is Madison, who has an entrepreneurial spirit if ever I saw one. She is of African-American descent and very proud of her ancestral roots. She is being raised by her Mother, a very successful business lawyer. Madison shovels driveways in winter and mows lawns in summer. She was tempted once to cheat her customers, but we had a long talk about it, and she realizes now that honesty will always pay off in the long run.

One of my favorite friends is Tommy. He's another anomaly (don't you just love that word?) because he comes off as grumpy and rude, but he's a pushover for any kind of animal. I think he's afraid of showing emotion, that it will make him look weak, but kindness is a strength, not a weakness. It takes much more guts to stand up for the right things than it does to just bow down or give in. Right?

The others—Thad, Simon, Natty, Phillip, and Andy—make up our little "band of buddies" and we look out for each other.

Noises and feet rustling against fallen leaves makes me open my eyes and jerk the ear buds out. *Sorry, Wolfgang, the present calls.*

"I hate coming out here," Maggie grumbled.

"Well, it's a good thing you're not a hunter. You make a lot of noise."

Trying to be patient, I give her my best smile. "But hey, you're the one demanding privacy, remember?"

She rebuked me with a dramatic roll of her eyes that made me want to warn her that they could get stuck that way. I resisted the urge to sound like my grandmother.

"Jaycee, if you had a smart phone like the rest of the world, then you wouldn't need that old cd player strapped to your waist. And there are private places to talk other than the spooky woods."

"I know. But I like the way CDs sound. Like my dad likes records, and my grandma likes the horn thing. Especially in the woods. So, what's up?"

"You like being limited to twenty songs? Jaycee, I can have thousands of songs on my phone. *Thousands*!"

She held up her phone as if I could see all her songs pouring out and onto the grass.

"And how many of those thousands of songs do you *actually* listen to? Thirty?"

She just shook her head like I was crazy and began prancing around the log and me as if she were floating on air. Her green eyes seemed brighter, her red hair more stark and brilliant.

"Electronics aside, what's your big announcement then? You seem a lot more chipper than normal."

"Chipper? What are you? Fifty? Besides, I'm always happy, Jaycee. You know that!"

"Relax," I said, gesturing with my hands as if to take her fleeting fancies down a few feet. "I'm just teasing you. I know you're always happy. So what's going on? Why the secrecy?"

Maggie staggered around the fallen log, as only someone could who was completely fish-out-of-water uncomfortable being in the woods. I could see the sharp edge of one of her canines nibbling at her lower lip. It was an irresistibly cute trait she had, among several I often found annoying. She glanced up at me, a coy smile wrestled with her face. "I did it, Jaycee. I really just did it!"

She blurted out the news, whatever it was as yet unrevealed, catching herself and then coming to a fervent whisper. She raised her eyebrows waiting for me to respond.

But, she received nothing from me except a very confused smile. "You did what, Mags? Got a good grade?" I toyed with her. Maggie was a notoriously bad student. Well, grade-wise, she did fine. There were always boys willing to do her work for her. But, when it came to her applying herself—not so much.

She tilted her head toward me, raising her eyebrows higher, and whispered, "You know. It. I . . . we *did* it."

Her face turned feverish with excitement—and something else, too, but I wasn't sure what—as she realized I had figured out what she had done. The real problem swimming around in my head was who with, and I didn't have to wait long to find out.

"Joshua!" she announced, answering the unspoken question.

"Oh," I sneered, unable to hide my displeasure. "Joshua."

I resisted the urge to poke my finger down my throat and gag. That she hooked with him was disappointing to say the least.

Maggie's excitement quickly fell away as she saw my face drop. "You're such a prude, Jaycee. I can't believe I even told you. I knew how you would react. You're always judging me. Always!"

I didn't respond. I go to great lengths never to judge her or anyone else. It's not my place. I want to tell myself that I didn't say anything because Maggie needed to vent her problems, and I was just being a good friend. I want to say I was just hearing her out, trying to see things from her point of view and not allowing my personal emotions to conflict with what happened with what appeared to be a happy occasion for her. Yet I know none of those excuses were honest. I didn't respond because I couldn't respond. I was weak from my toes to my knees, and at any moment, I could fall right over.

It was up to Maggie when to lose her own virginity. It wasn't up to me or anybody else for that matter. I know she'd been wanting to for a long time. She had told me she felt like an outsider with our friends. Losing her virginity was a rite of passage for her. It was a way of saying, "Hey, world, I'm here, and I am a woman." For me it was much different. I needed to wait. I wanted my first time to be special.

46

And frankly, Joshua wasn't special enough. Not for my friend, not for me, probably not for any girl. He had a lot going for him, but I was having a hard time hiding my disappointment in her actions.

"I'm not judging you, Maggie!" My voice came out as a scream. It was so much louder than I had ever expected it to be, and yet it was there like a shrill banshee.

Maggie turned away from me.

"I'm sorry, Mags. I didn't mean to."

I chased after her as she started slowly jogging away from me. "Maggie, wait. Wait! Just wait!" I caught up to her and grabbed her by the shoulder.

She spun around to face me, tears streaming down her cheeks. "Wait for what? You to give me some lecture on what it's like to be the Perfect Miss Priss? Like you? No, thanks. If I want a lecture, I'll go to my parents!"

She turned away again.

"Maggie, please wait!" I cried after her. "I'm not upset. Not at all. I'm happy for you. I just . . . you just surprised me is all. I had no idea you were going to, then you did, and you told me. I just didn't know what to say. It was a little overwhelming for me. I'm so sorry. I didn't mean anything by it. Just shocked, that's all."

Maggie stopped walking away, and I caught up to her. I put my arms around her, tight, taking hold as if we were friends who hadn't seen each other in years. Then she hugged me back. Tears soaked my face, her hair, and I could only imagine I was crying as hard as Maggie.

She whispered in my ear, "Thank you, Jaycee."

Then she paused, and took a deep breath. "But, I didn't have sex. I was just joking."

She let go of me, and playfully shoved me.

"You're joking?" I confirmed. "That was all just some elaborate joke then?"

"Mm-hmm." She nodded, and a twinkle came into her eye. "I had to know how you would react. What if I do one day, and it sucks? What if I need you like that and you over react? What if I just need your blessing, or comfort, and you treat me like a child."

47

"I don't know what to say. I'm happy, I guess. But, why did you think you needed to trick me, or test me or something. Why couldn't you just say, 'Hey, if I tell you this how would you react?'"

"Don't be silly. You would never react that way. You would make something up to make me feel good about it. But, I don't know how you'll react when you're emotional. No one knows how anyone will react."

Maggie wasn't wrong. I didn't know how I would react. In fact, at this moment as I held her, I didn't know how I felt. I still had the clutching sense of pain in my chest as if Maggie had actually lost her virginity. It was crazy, and I didn't know how to react had it been true. Yes, Maggie was right. I didn't agree with her testing me, it felt somehow disloyal, but I understood what she was saying. I know she resented my lectures about being a good person. I just have a hard time with how she sometimes does things. To me, it is easier to avoid trouble in the first place than it is to clean up after a mistake. Still, as I held Maggie and could feel the warmth of her body, I had a sense that something was not entirely right. Something had happened. Maybe it wasn't sex, but it was something.

"What do you suppose they're doing?" Maggie let go of me and walked toward the edge of the bluff, pointing below.

The sight was more curious than anything. Five large flatbed tractor-trailer rigs were driving down the winding road heading toward Serenity from the north. A convoy. It was dark, and we could only see their headlights poking through the night, leading their way forward. As they passed under the occasional streetlight, the dark trailers could be seen outlined in reflective paint. The trailers would normally have held coal, or soil, maybe even logs. But the trailers were just open and empty rectangles.

"I don't know." I replied. "Looks weird though. Have you ever seen that many trucks even come into town?"

"Not unless it was a garbage truck. Definitely not one of those flat things. Those are huge!"

"Yeah. I wonder what they're building then?"

"Or taking away." Sadness showed in the way the words came out.

"What do you mean?" I asked her.

Just like the hug she'd given me a short minute ago, I could tell there was much more behind her words, than what she'd actually said.

Maggie looked at me. Then her eyes darted away. "Oh, Jaycee. I don't know if I should be the one to say anything. I mean. I don't even know if I know for sure. I've just heard stuff."

"What kind of stuff?"

She stepped back over to the log and sat down. "You know how people talk. My dad was talking to his stockbroker about some store coming into town. Kind of a big store . . . a *Whalemart*."

As she said the name of the notorious big-box retail chain with the cute little blue whale logo, her voice dropped to a mere whisper. It was as if she thought they were listening. But I knew her whisper came from the fact that a Whalemart would surely destroy my own dad's business. My dad owns the only hardware store in town. He is everything to this town, and more. Even when he was having problems of his own, he has provided for others who couldn't pay their bills, like loaning them tools instead of them having to buy them. It probably wasn't the most profitable way to run a business, but it is *his* way of running *his* business. He believes you have to be loyal to your customers, in good times and bad.

"Nah, that can't be true. What would they want with a town as small as Serenity? There's not another town for fifty miles. They'd hardly be able to get enough people to work there, let alone shop there. Can't be."

Maggie just shrugged, but her face told me all I needed to know. Of course, people would shop there. They might love my dad, but when it came to low prices, Whalemart couldn't be beat. It certainly couldn't be beat by my dad, who couldn't stock his shelves with vast quantities like the big chain stores could. "Quality over quantity," he liked to say. But what people want these days is cheap.

It wasn't the easiest news to take, but I'd find out the truth first before I started getting all freaked out. Dad would tell me. My family didn't keep secrets from one another. His store was fine. I was just there the day before, and he was as happy as could be. There wasn't a sign at all that anything was wrong, and Dad couldn't exactly keep things like that a secret. His face would tell it all.

"I'm sure it's just rumors, Mags. I haven't heard anything definite at all."

She stretched out her long legs, and I couldn't help but be a little jealous of how beautiful she is. Her phone dinged, and she took it out of her pocket. She glanced at the screen and giggled. Then tapped something quickly on the screen and giggled again.

She glanced up at me. "It's Joshua. He can be so funny sometimes."

"Joshua?"

"Yeah, Jaycee. You should give him a chance. I think you'd like him."

"But he's such a perv. He can hardly go a minute without talking about his . . . you know."

Maggie laughed out loud. "I know. I know. It's funny though. At least I think it's kind of cute."

"Well, whatever. We should probably get back anyway. If I stay out too long, my parents will freak out at me."

"Mine will just ask why I came home so early."

And Maggie wasn't joking either. Her parents weren't exactly what you would call nurturing people. Whatever a dollar could buy, they would buy it for Maggie. Anything to avoid interacting with her.

Maggie grabbed her phone again. She read a new message and then typed away with her thumbs, the neon polish flashing in the dark. "Yeah, we should probably go."

At the moment, I'd completely forgotten about those trucks we'd just seen heading toward town. They were an odd sight for us to see but not so strange as seeing something like a leprechaun lingering at the edge of the woods.

Besides, they are harmless, right? At least according to old Mr. Sweeny's stories. At least that's what I've always thought.

And that was when we heard the sirens.

Chapter 7

Soccer is a magical game.

—David Beckham

Two weeks ago . . .

For years to come, we would call it The Big Game. Our soccer team, the Winds, had never ever in the whole history of the school been to the state playoffs. But, for some reason, we all clicked our senior year, and most of players were seniors. Our record was 22-3, currently the best in state, and defeating our cross-county rivals Meadowlands meant that we would officially be in the state tournament. Sure, it was a matter of a technicality. But, for a school who'd never been to state, this was a big deal. With half a dozen games left in our regular season, we could clinch our conference today.

Before the game started, the twelve of us stood along the sidelines, including Johnny, who was our so-called team manager, but functioned as our water boy. He was good at it too, and proud of what he did. As we all stood shoulder to shoulder, I'd never felt so proud. The coming year will be filled with some of the biggest challenges I've ever faced. We are graduating in only a few short months, I still have a college to choose, and I'll likely be saying goodbye to my friends for months, if not permanently. I am not so naïve or flighty as to think our current friendships are meant to last a lifetime. I've even wondered about the close friendships I have with Johnny, Maggie, Judith, and if they will stand the test of time.

Meadowlands—the players, coaches, and a lot of fans decked out in team colors—stand across the field from us. Like us, Meadowlands barely has enough players to substitute even one person during the course of the game. When we have played big city schools, they prac-

51

tically send in an entire team for each substitution. I took the fact that Meadowlands didn't have a huge numbers advantage over us as a good thing. We call ourselves "small but mighty" and take pride in our ability to outlast other larger teams. It has taught us to work and fight harder for the win. I never felt like I had fresh legs. I always felt like I was sprinting up a hill, with no option to stop.

"You ready for this?" Maggie nudged me in the side. "Today, we do it. I need to play well today. I heard UW is going to have someone here. An actual scout."

Maggie is one of about five girls on the team likely to go to a Division One college on a soccer scholarship. I'm not one of them. To tell the truth, I've always been the glue that holds things together, but not the best player by any stretch. I am great on offense, not so great on defense, where I'm barely above average. My best trait is keeping my teammates from fighting all the time. It wasn't as if they fought more than anyone else, it's just that I was good at keeping down any infighting. In a strange way, I function as the Winds' parent. Not a glorious role, but a role nonetheless.

Maggie has been pining for universities to come out and watch us for the better part of the year. Her dad sent out dozens of letters with her stats and interest. She'd chosen University of Wisconsin, but as far as we knew, UW hadn't yet sent anyone out to look at her. Today would be the first day. And as Maggie mentioned the words to me, behind us, two men in suits came walking up and sat down on the bleachers. One of them had a large professional camera hanging around his neck.

I nudged Maggie and rolled my eyes toward the bleachers. "Better play good today. I think you're right."

Maggie started bouncing on her toes as if warming up, but I think it was more to calm her jitters than anything.

"We're gonna do this today. And, in a couple weeks, we'll have a nice fancy trophy to finish off our last year of high school."

The refs blew a whistle and the Winds formed up in a circle. Our chant started as a whisper . . . *Winds*. Then it slowly grew, "Winds. *Winds*. *Winds*. Let's go, Winds!"

With that, we all took a stutter step forward and like an explosion, our arms ripped backwards, and we all pretended to be thrown from our feet and away from each other. Our pregame battle cry had become newsworthy throughout the state as reporters had captured us in various photos exploding backwards and to the ground. It was almost as famous as our current winning streak of twenty games.

Our jerseys are purple and white. Near the end of the first period, mine is decorated with splashes of red; blood stains from my last goal, which sent me sliding into the goalie and the back of the net along with the ball. I ignored the tingling pain, knowing it would soon dissipate as the match wears on. To say our match against Meadowlands is a rivalry would be as much an understatement as saying this game didn't mean anything, or would have been easy. Truth of the matter is that this game is one of the hardest I have ever played. Despite my quiet and laid-back attitude off the field, I am aggressive on the field. Like I said, I am not as skilled a player as some of my teammates, but I am the hardest working. During this game, I've practically been a machine chasing after everything. I've been given two verbal warnings for slide-tackling, and I nearly knocked myself unconscious diving for a header. I probably looked possessed to the coaches and fans.

I was pulled off the field for a breather by my coach. "Put a cold rag on your nose, Jaycee. You're bleeding."

"Hi, Jaycee." Johnny handed me with a paper cup filled with water. "Here is water for you, Jaycee. You need to stay hydro-lated. Water is important, Jaycee."

I smiled at Johnny's ability to make up words, grabbed a towel and a few ice chips, and held it against my nose. "Thanks, Johnny. How are you doing today? I haven't had a chance to talk to you."

"I am good, Jaycee."

"Have your parents figured out what to do with your Grandma?"

"No. They fight a lot, Jaycee."

As always, he spoke matter-of-factly with no emotion.

"I'm sorry to hear that. Maybe you should come with us to the party next week. I bet you'd have fun. I'm not a big party person either, but Jaime's grandfather will be there. He's supposed to be a descendant of Crazy Horse. Remember him from history class? You might enjoy talking to him. Maybe he can give you advice or something."

Johnny didn't react, but strangely he looked over to where the two strangers had been sitting on the bleachers. They were gone, but the simple fact that Johnny had looked over there made me realize there was something more to them than being college recruiters. My thoughts strayed from the game, *I wonder what is going on. I'd ask Johnny, but I don't think he would say anything. He isn't one to start gossip on a hunch. He's more of a facts person.*

"Thanks for the water. I feel better now."

Johnny took my cup, and within minutes, I went back in the game, but I can't stop thinking about those men. Were they here scouting players, or potential customers for *Whalemart*? For sure, they are different from anyone I've ever seen in Serenity. They had just stood there watching, not seeming to root for either team, snapping the occasional photo from the camera the taller of the two men was sporting. I knew they weren't here for me. Why would they be? But still, they made me feel as if I was doing something wrong and they were PI's collecting evidence against me. It was awkward. That didn't make any sense though. Of course, neither did two men in suits watching a high school soccer match and taking photos, unless they were college scouts.

Anyway, it doesn't matter now. We are tied with Meadowlands, and there isn't much time left in regulation play. I need to get my head in the game!

The team huddled together after scoring a goal. We have to act fast to win during regulation play, and not go into overtime. I look up at Judith Johnson, or as everyone called her, JJ. "You ready for this?"

JJ nodded vehemently—too winded to speak—and I knew it was true. JJ was the best right wing in the entire state. She has a cross that no one can beat.

Maggie came running and joined us in the huddle. She's been on the other side of the field, hobbling badly. "I'm here. What are we doing? What's the play?"

I give Maggie my best smile. I love that girl. I was surprised we hadn't so much as mentioned the previous night. Usually, we joke about everything. Last night already seems like it will be an inside joke the rest of our lives. In fact, all day at school, Maggie hadn't brought up anything at all, and I was too uncomfortable to bring it up myself.

"A full on drive down the right side. JJ will cross from the corner. I'll take the ball and you back me up."

"Jaycee. Let me take the last shot." She glanced around, eventually catching sight of the two men, now on top of the hill. "It's important to me to get this one."

"But, that side's not your best."

"I don't care. I want this one."

I shrugged. "Sure, Mags. Take it, I'll back you up."

"Will do, Cap," Maggie said, smiling at me as if the idea had been mine from the start.

"Okay, on two!" I yelled out, "One . . . Two . . ." And simultaneously, the entire team loudly drew out, "Go, Winds!"

As everyone jogs to their place on the field I risk a glance up at the men on the hill.

"I saw them too," Maggie says, as she comes up behind me. "I hope JJ is on with her pass. I need this one to secure a scholarship."

While she *said* she needs a scholarship, what Maggie really meant was she wants to secure a place on the team. Money isn't a problem for Maggie's parents who toss money at her like rose petals. UW is known to be lax on tryouts for the girls who come in with a full scholarship. For Maggie, it's a matter of bragging rights. She'd rather earn a place on the team than feel like her parents bought her one. I get that.

"I saw them taking pictures," I said.

"Of me?" Maggie whispered, and I shrugged. "Well, they are either scouts or well-dressed pervs."

We both laughed.

Meadowlands starts with the ball, and before their center realizes it, Maggie darts forward and takes advantage of a short pass that misses the mark. She uses the heel of her foot to tap the ball back to me. I slide the ball between my legs and then up the field just as the center slides to try and knock it out of my control. I loft the ball to JJ, who is sprinting down the sideline.

As I sprint forward, I can't help but notice another man walking along the hillside and extending a hand out to the two men in suits. The third man is in a suit too, although slightly more flamboyant than the somber black of the other two. I realize quickly that the man in the light blue suit is Serenity's mayor, and my friend Judith's father.

My head is bouncing in and out of the game, which I know is not good, but I can't help wondering what the mayor has to do with these guys? Why does he seem so comfortable with them? I'm getting a sneaking suspicion that these men are not here for the game at all. But what else could it be? Then another shock: Father Paul, wearing a windbreaker jacket and baseball cap—I still recognized his gait, even at a distance—joined the three men.

Before I could process that strange occurrence, I was jolted back into the game play.

I let myself play on autopilot, sprinting forward, trying to lag a couple paces behind Maggie, JJ, and the ball. JJ is swarmed by Meadowlands' players almost as soon as she gains control of the ball. Luckily, she is able to tap the ball between the legs of a Meadowlands' player, then with a brilliant spin move, she gets back in control and ahead of the group. She'll have to stop at some point, and everyone knows that as soon as she does, she will be swarmed again, making the winning kick all the more difficult.

I look up again. The mayor takes an envelope from one of the men, sticks it in his pocket, and is now laughing despite the straight faces of the other two men. He raises his arm and points, drawing an imaginary line from one side of the field to the other, as if he's showing the men something. Somehow, this looks like a business transaction; I don't think they're sports scouts. I think they just bought a politician.

Father Paul, I see, near them, and he is looking at the field, his gaze searching for me, I think. We locked eyes for a split second, and I swear he looked . . . frightened.

When I look back at the field, JJ is in the corner of the field. She glances toward me, and for only a fraction of a moment, I feel as if JJ knows something about the men observing us from above the field. It's like she wants to tell me what they're doing, but something is holding her back. We aren't as close as we once were, but we're still good friends. In fact, only Johnny and Maggie are closer to me, which may play a role in why JJ has been so quiet as of late.

Meadowlands swarmed on JJ. Big mistake, as with a couple of perfectly timed taps, she spins herself free, leaving only two players to defend against the inevitable pass to Maggie. Once JJ is free from the pack, she gives the ball a slight tap forward, and with a long stride and swooping kick, she sends the ball cross field nearly perfectly.

Maggie is now perfectly lined up with the ball, and a wide smile lights up her face as she must have just realized how easy it will be to tap the ball into the goal. It is all about timing. The Meadowlands' goalie has been hovering around the right side of the net all day, and Maggie had commented on how she knew the left side would be an easy target for her. That's where it fell apart. Maggie is too excited and as she sprints forward she slips on the grass, sprawling forward, sliding on her chest.

By the time Maggie recovers from her fall, it's too late for her to finish off the play. I feel myself going on autopilot again, sprinting forward, and knowing exactly where I'm going to head the ball into the goal. I didn't expect the goalie to run out in front of me and try to deflect or grab the ball. The entire game, the goalie had hidden within the net as if she were a scared mouse burrowed into her hole. Suddenly, she was aggressive.

I watched as if in slo-mo as her hands reached out to grab the ball, something caused her to mistime her step, and instead of the ball going into her hands, it deflected through them, allowing the ball to launch higher yet. I readjusted my speed and aligned with the ball. I had to move faster toward the goal to even get to the ball, but without any defenders remaining, I had an open net.

In two long strides and with all the strength left remaining in my legs, I launched. My head made contact with the ball. Between the time the ball passed through the goal and my head smacked into the goal's metal frame, I caught the last glimpse of the men on the hill above me. One was holding a camera, which appeared to snap at just the time I hit the metal frame. It was truly an out-of-body experience. I watched myself sail through the air, smack the ball with my head, and then crashed into the frame, almost as though it was me looking through the camera lens.

I heard the team and the crowd erupt as we pulled out another close one against Meadowlands. The whistle blew just as I slammed into the ground. My teammates piled on me in excitement. When I looked up, the men, including the mayor and Father Paul, were gone. There was something ominous, but I couldn't quite grasp what it was.

Once my teammates got off me and made their way toward the bench, I stood up, hobbled, and stumbled forward. I was dizzy and unable to control myself. *Something is happening. Something bad . . . is . . . happening. I can't control my steps. My feet won't move right.*

I see Maggie and stumble toward her, collapsing against her body. She has a scowl on her face and shoves me off. What have I done wrong?

A few more stumbling steps and I collapse to the ground, feeling like a strong hand is pushing me down, against my will. The only thought that echoes through my mind, in a quiet whisper that repeats itself like a broken record skipping on the needle, *Let it happen . . . Let it happen . . . Let it happen . . .* And then there was nothing.

Chapter 8

All good is hard. All evil is easy. Dying, losing, cheating,
and mediocrity is easy. Stay away from easy.
—Scott Alexander

By the time I woke up, the team was gathered around me, huddled behind a couple of paramedics. "She'll need to see her doctor," one of them said. "I think it's probably a concussion."

I didn't know how long I'd been out, but Meadowlands had long since left on their team bus. Johnny was standing closest to me as I was lifted onto my feet. In the distance, I could see Maggie walking off by herself toward the locker room. She was tapping something into her phone as usual. Then vertigo hit again, and everything was spinning. I closed my eyes and tried to yell out to Maggie, but the words wouldn't come, and before I knew it, I had succumbed to the lightness growing within me.

I woke up again, this time in the hospital. My journal was laying open on my chest. My parents must have brought it, and surprisingly, I'd written something in chicken scratch that only slightly resembled my handwriting. I couldn't recall anything that happened after I fell for the last time on the field.

"My head hurts," I said to whoever might be listening.

Then my world went dark again.

Next time I woke up, my parents were hovering, one on each side of my bed. I must have hit the goal post pretty hard because the last thing I remember was hearing a strange white squirrel talking to me. Seriously, it was talking to me. Like, I could even understand it.

"Let it happen," is what the squirrel said, repeatedly. I don't know what it was talking about, but if it was talking about letting myself pass out from bleeding in my brain, I don't know how I would not have let that happen. It's not like I had a choice in the matter.

As I had slipped into darkness, I thought about Maggie, how she walked away from me, and so when I finally woke up in the hospital, Maggie was also the person I was thinking about. I have to admit that I was a little bummed my parents were the only ones in the room with me. I was hoping to see my whole team, especially Maggie. But, my dad told me the hospital would only allow my parents. I guess it was a relief that others had at least tried.

What is it about that squirrel? I had no idea what I'd meant by seeing and hearing a squirrel. I must have really been out of it. I looked up at my dad. "Did Maggie come by?"

He shook his head. "But Father Paul came to see you. I stepped out, but I think he said a prayer over you, and then he left. He said to tell you he's sorry."

I wanted to ask if he had seen a white squirrel either at the ball field or in my hospital room, but instantly knew that would be a bad idea. "Father Paul is sorry? Sorry for what?"

"Beats me," Dad said. "Don't shoot the messenger, Jaycee."

He gave me a feeble smile.

As to Maggie, what had I done to her? The image of her walking away from me was haunting, even though everyone else was around me. My parents were sitting in chairs close to each other, holding hands. Both of them looked as if they had been crying for hours with bright and wet faces of tears, worry, and sweat.

"Hey, you guys cheer up," I croaked, my throat dry and raspy. "I'll be all right. It doesn't feel that bad. You don't need to worry."

"We know, honey," Mom said to me.

My dad didn't look up.

It dawned on me that it wasn't worry about me causing them to cry. There was something else going on. Something much worse than their only daughter laying in a hospital bed with a concussion.

What was happening?

The doctor came into my room breaking the tension. He began by apologizing for the hospital's old, outdated equipment, and wishing the tests they needed to do could be done quicker. "Sorry, folks, but the town just refused to invest in this little hospital. We're doing the best we can with what we have." He then added, "But you can go home for now. If anything comes back abnormal, we'll call you in for another consult. Take it easy, kid." He walked out of my room, and I was getting dressed before the door shut.

My parents, as well as school authorities, had declared I couldn't come back for several days due to my concussion. My headaches had gone away though, and the last few days of a week away from school were slowly becoming boring, even for me; someone who didn't mind being alone.

I think the worst part is that I haven't heard from Maggie in all this time. I texted her a few times, but those messages went unanswered. I knew she had seen the texts because her phone never left her hand. That's a fact. Maggie was ignoring me, and for some reason, I can't figure out. What did I do wrong?

Mom and Dad had finally started back working at the store. The first couple days neither would leave the house; afraid something would happen to me while they were gone. But, finally, they couldn't hold out anymore and had to get back to their daily lives. Besides, I hadn't had any problems for at least seventy-two hours. The doctor had even said I was probably clear, and except for a follow up appointment, I was likely fine. I picked up the bottle of Percocet the doctor prescribed me.

I was surprised too, but the narcotics were only in case of extreme pain and as a precaution. I hadn't even bothered to open the bottle. I shook it and listened to the pills bounce around the small orange container. The bottle made a better musical instrument to appease my time than the pills were of value to me. I placed the container on my nightstand just as the doorbell rang.

"Ugh!" I said.

My mind seemed a little blurry, but otherwise fine. My body on the other hand was achy and exhausted. I got up, put on my slippers, and walked to the front door.

My day brightened when I opened the door and saw Father Paul standing there, and his gold-etched leather Bible in hand. Each finger on both his hands had a unique and ornate ring ranging from silver to gold and I would guess platinum. Each ring, of course, was laden with a cross, some etched in the ring's metal, and others encrusted in various bright jewels. It only reminded me of our previous conversation, but I also understood the rings could signify accomplishments within the church or were gifts from people Father Paul had helped in the past. And there were a lot of people he'd helped.

He was dressed well, but not in his priestly garb as I would have expected outside the school. Yet, I do distinctly remember a conversation with Father Paul a year ago when he said he wears his church clothes the way everyone else does—during mass. I laughed then, and I couldn't help but chuckle to myself a bit now as he stood there, dapperly dressed, and quite unlike the priest you would see in a movie.

"Jaycee. How's my favorite student?"

"You're not supposed to have a favorite, Father."

I acted shocked, but I was flattered and not really surprised. Father Paul and I had had a great relationship since the first day I stepped into his office asking questions about God and church. Over the years, I'm sure there have been thousands of similar questions.

He couldn't hold his smile back. *Such a smart girl*, I'm sure he was thinking. "How are you feeling, Jaycee. Better, I hear?"

"Yes, much better. Thank you for coming by. Would you like to come in?"

He nodded. Being as tall as he is, I can only assume Father Paul ducks frequently, otherwise it was a God thing. He crossed the threshold of the front door as I held it open, and dipped his head to his chest as if blessing the home as he entered.

"I spoke with your father today. He seemed in good spirits."

"He always is," I lied a bit.

Dad had changed in the last couple of days since my injury. But, it was good to hear his façade wasn't showing to anyone other than me.

"I had to run by his store to grab painting supplies."

"Oh! Are you painting your house? Office?"

He let out a burst of laughter, "Sorry, Jaycee. I am about as useless as a fish on a bicycle when it comes to anything requiring manual labor. Both of my parents were professors, and it wasn't in any of our blood to manually do anything. I'm afraid to say, I adopted their traits. I've hired a couple of men to help paint the rectory and maybe my office."

"Ah, I see. I need to grab something real quick. Have a seat, Father. I'll be right back."

All I really needed to do was change my clothes and put on some socks. I was still in my pajamas, embarrassingly showing off my love of puppies. It felt weird.

"I'll just wait here then."

I changed quickly into jeans and a clean flannel shirt. I slid on some socks and plucked my journals from my bed, then returned them to the shelf. Before I went back to Father Paul, I grabbed the pills from my nightstand and threw them in my pocket. I didn't want Father Paul to accidentally see them and question me. Despite never doing drugs before, it was never good for an adult to think there was a possibility. Even prescription pills.

"Okay, I'm back! Sorry, I'd just been in those clothes for a few days, and I felt awkward looking sloppy in front of you."

"Oh, don't worry about that."

He had chosen Dad's lounge chair, I saw.

"Can I get you a drink?"

"No, it's okay. Thank you, though. I am only here to check on you and make sure you are okay. I know you're a student, but I also consider you a friend. I understand it can be a little . . . strange? I guess that would be the best word—a little strange for a priest to call a student a friend. With all of the conversations we've had, I don't know what else to call you. I see myself as somewhat of a mentor. If that makes sense?"

"Yeah, of course. I see it the same way. I'm happy you came by."

I walked over to the kitchen to grab myself a soda. The pills in my pocket began to rattle with each step.

"The other thing I wanted to talk to you about the other day is our conversation."

I closed the refrigerator, and snapped open the can, which let out a burst of air, like a steam locomotive. "Oh? I didn't think much about it once I left."

I'd rather hear you explain why you were talking to those men at the soccer game.

"Yes, that's probably true. But, I still feel like I owe you an apology. You see, I was not being completely honest with you. Or, I should say I was not being completely honest with myself. You were right. I do enjoy the finer things in life. I enjoy my collections. While I still believe my intent is good, and what I said about investments is true, I don't believe I was fully honest."

I didn't expect him to just come right out and say it. In fact, I never thought I'd hear Father Paul say he was sorry. Certainly not for his actions. That is, he rarely made mistakes enough to justify apologizing. However, I could see what I said was a personal attack and in many ways, I may have owed him an apology, rather than it being the other way around.

"Well, you don't need to—"

He gestured me to stop with a wave of his hand. "Yes, I do need to apologize."

I walked into the room where he was sitting. The pills still bouncing around in my pocket. The noise seemed to trigger something in him.

"Did your doctor prescribe you something?"

There it was, the words I was terrified of hearing from an adult. I stopped and took a calming breath.

"Yes. He prescribed Percocet. I haven't taken any though." I took the bottle from my pocket and tossed it to him. "I'm not big on medication."

He smiled. "That's a good trait." He shook the bottle between two fingers as though it were a suspect bug that might bite him. "Not everyone has that kind of discipline."

I blushed a little. He placed the bottle of Percocet on the table next to the chair.

"Well, that's all I really wanted to talk to you about. I wanted to check on you and make sure to apologize. I figured both demanded a personal visit. I hope that is all right?"

"Oh, of course. I appreciate it. But you really didn't have—"

He waved my comment away again. "Yes, Jaycee, I did."

He stood up and walked to the door. "I can see myself out. I hope to see you in school bright and early Monday morning. I'm sure you'll be feeling back to normal in no time."

I thanked him and closed the door as he walked down our long sidewalk and to his car.

I spent the rest of the day in my room, stretched out on my bed, staring at the ceiling, and contemplating the difference between greed and appreciation for beautiful things.

The clock chimed six, and I heard my dad walk up the stairs. He poked his head in my bedroom door looking exhausted.

"How was business today?" I asked. "You look tired."

He didn't respond immediately, but nodded at me politely. "I'm hungry. How about you? Pizza tonight? Your mom should be home soon. She'll probably want the Hawaiian."

"That's fine. Always like a little pizza for dinner. But I'd rather have pepperoni than ham. 'Kay?"

Dad was a taller than average man, much like Father Paul. He had light brown hair that was cleanly cut short, yet he still sported the 1990s sideburns made so popular by the television show *Beverly Hills 90210*. I'd seen the reruns before, and knew what my mom was talking about when she said those sideburns still make her go, *"Oooh la la."* Years of hard labor gave him a chiseled look with a strong jaw and broad shoulders. Mom was pretty in her own right, but I always wondered if she was jealous at the way other women would look at Dad.

"So how was your day then? You enjoy playing hooky?"

"As much as I can." That was true. I didn't mind being home from school. I didn't need to know the local gossip the way that Maggie did. I was as comfortable being home on my own, as I was being with . . . well, let's face it, I preferred being by myself more than being around crowds of people.

"Work was good. Stayed busy all day. Father Paul stopped by for a few minutes."

"He came by here too."

"Oh yeah? What did he want?" Dad paused a moment, and looked like he was thinking on his own question. Before I could answer he said, "Oh, yeah, I do remember him saying something about wanting to check up on you. Said he was worried and sorry he hadn't already stopped by. He's a good man."

I could see storm clouds rolling in from the west. They were dark and full, ready to drop a barrage of rain on us. "Weird, I didn't know it was supposed to rain today. Did you?"

Dad walked over to the window. "No. I guess not. I'm going to go and collect the chairs outside so they don't go bouncing around the neighborhood. You mind ordering the pizza?"

"Okay." The storms appeared to be rolling in fast. *Poor delivery guy,* I thought, just as I noticed a small white squirrel playing in the branches of our sycamore tree. *Never saw a white one. Sure is cute.* "Stay safe, little guy," I said, eyeing the roiling clouds and watching him darting in and out of a hole in the tree.

I pulled out my old flip phone and snapped a quick picture. The resolution wasn't great, and the photo was grainy. I thought about Maggie's super fancy smart phone. *Yeah, I suppose her fancy phone has a couple cool things. Like taking great pics of a cute white squirrel.*

"Be safe, lil guy," I blessed him, then went to call for a pizza.

Mom was home before the storm hit, and only a minute before the pizza guy came running up to the house to avoid the first of what would be a major torrential downpour. We sat in front of the television to watch a show while we ate, the typical Woods' tradition. But, before the show started, Dad clicked the TV off.

"I need to tell you both something," he said, around a mouthful of pizza.

His tone wasn't exactly joyful, if you catch my drift. He let out a long sigh, one I remember well from such news as both of my grandparents passing away, and not getting the dog my parents had promised me for an entire year. Whatever his news was, I knew from that dramatic sigh it wasn't going to be good.

Mom didn't say anything, but by her unsurprised reaction, I could tell she already had a heads-up on what was happening. Meaning, I was the only one in the family who was not in the loop. Nothing new there. I guess like all parents, they always wanted to protect me from times when the real world gets too real for a "kid".

"I'm not going to beat around the bush here," he said.

I don't think either Mom, nor I thought he would. Dad wasn't exactly someone who messed around when it came to serious business. I remember once when I was fourteen, Maggie and I were playing with aerosol spray and a lighter we found on the sidewalk. It was really just me doing it. For all the predicaments Maggie had gotten me into, I was the culprit that day. Anyway, Dad found us. He marched us both right over to Maggie's parent's house and explained what he found us doing. He also explained that I was the only one he saw doing something, and that I should know better. I also had to apologize. Despite being angry with him, it wasn't until I told Father Paul about what had happened that I realized how good of a dad my dad really was. If anything helped, it was the admiration of honesty I saw in Father Paul's eyes when he said, "Your father truly is a great man, Jaycee. I hope you realize that. Most men would have hidden the truth for fear of being called a bad father. Your father stood up to his fears, and despite what others may have thought, he put himself out there."

So, when Dad stood in front of Mom and I, he was dead serious. His smile held the same reassuring warmth it always did, but his feelings were betrayed by his eyes.

"The mayor stopped into the store today"—he looked at me—"shortly before Father Paul. In fact, I think Father Paul may have overheard our conversation."

A flash of lightning following by a crackle *boom* of thunder shook the house as if ominously framing this conversation.

"I don't know for sure, but we may lose the store. In fact, we may lose the whole shopping mall. The mayor was telling me that Whalemart has been aggressively buying up land in the area, and with the exception of the strip mall . . ." He looked at me again. "Including Sister Kristen's shelter, they are close to being able to claim imminent domain, and that would eventually lead to building a large Whalemart store in the middle of town. Even if I were somehow able to keep my store, a store like Whalemart would run us out of business, and fast."

I didn't say anything. With tears falling from my eyes, it was all I could do to control my frustration. I didn't understand what was going on around town. Maggie was mad at me, Johnny's parents were sending his grandmother to a nursing home, and now Dad was about to lose his store. He'd built the store from the ground up. He struggled through the bad years and successfully became known as the go-to hardware guy. Everyone loved him. How could the town let him lose everything like that? It was incomprehensible, as I guess all big life changes are when they happen.

An image popped into my head—the mayor putting an envelope in his pocket at the game. Whatever was in that envelope had made him smile. Was it money? A payoff from the Whalemart people for declaring imminent domain and taking land? I hated to think bad about people, but things weren't adding up.

"Is there nothing you can do, Joe?" Mom asked. "Nothing?"

"I'm afraid it's out of my hands. The mayor didn't seem very optimistic. Worse comes to worst and I will just end up working for the same company that puts me out of business. Best is that I somehow keep the store and fend off the competition. It would be hard, but maybe, just maybe, the town would side with me. The problem is that Whalemart will offer better pay, more jobs, and better prices. It's an uphill battle either way." Dad looked at me, his eyes lost. "You okay, honey?"

No, I wasn't okay. As long as I could remember, Dad had owned that store. I grew up with it. The store was my home as much as where we now sat because I was only four when he married my mom. I could feel the slight tremble in my arm, as if I were going to explode. Like a volcano inside me rumbling to get out. I couldn't believe what was happening to me. Everything seemed to be falling apart.

"I'm fine." I lied, not willing to let my parents know anything otherwise.

They had enough to worry about without worrying even more about me. I finished the remaining bite of my pizza crust and took the plate into the kitchen. "I think I'll just go to bed a little early. I'm not feeling great." I pointed to my head, "You know, the concussion and all."

"Maybe you should take a Percocet," Mom said. "I know you don't like taking medication, but I think you'd be surprised at how much it will help."

"Yeah, maybe." I glanced toward Dad's chair where I'd last seen Father Paul place the bottle of pills.

I walked over and couldn't see it on the table, or around the chair.

"You okay? What are you looking for?" Dad asked, laughing at my random search of his chair.

"Yeah, yeah. I'm just looking for . . . I guess I don't . . . Oh, never mind. I think I'm just going a bit crazy here."

The pills were gone. I'm sure I must have misplaced the bottle, but where did I put it? I kept replaying Father Paul looking at the pill bottle, then setting it down.

I went to bed feeling like a private detective with a mystery to solve. Who owned the land and the strip mall? It had always been one of those town secrets. If we could figure out who actually owns it, maybe we could form a group of citizens and pressure them not to sell to Whalemart. As I finally drifted off to sleep, my mind swerved to the party to celebrate going to the state tournament, planned for tomorrow. As averse as I am to parties, I wouldn't miss this one for all the concussions in the world.

Chapter 9

The bond with a true dog is as lasting as
the ties of this earth will ever be.

—Konrad Lorenz

Sister Kristen smiled as I walked into her office at Sister Kristen's Creature Comforts. She runs an animal rescue, mostly for dogs, but there were always several other types of animals, from bunnies to an actual mountain lion cub with an injured paw. Her place is at the end of the strip mall; my dad's hardware store is in the center. Like my dad, her rent was paid to a bookkeeper in the state capitol; some anonymous dude with a weird logo shaped like a pitchfork. At least that's what it looks like to me.

"How are you, dear? Father Paul told me you'd had a soccer accident."

Her voice carried the subtle yet guttural sound of her native Swedish. Sister Kristen is one of my favorite people. She is in her seventies, yet spry as a twenty-year-old. She's short, and her waist is slightly thicker than when I first met her three years ago. We met during a church retreat. She had taken us on a walk through the forest to find animals in their native habitats. While we never saw anything more than a few birds, I did learn a lot about how animals live. We found a few animal burrows, mole trails, an abandoned bear den, and I learned how to identify animal trails. It was the one sure way to find water, she said, if you followed them far enough.

I'd always had a connection to Sister Kristen, however different it was from my connection to Father Paul. Where Father Paul was a confidant, and someone who I would question about the church and theology, Sister Kristen was a mentor in many ways. I never had to ask her a question, or test her judgment. She was as close to a symbol of the Virgin Mary as I could imagine. She intuitively asked me questions, gave me guidance, and somehow always knew when something bothered me. But, she never pried. If I didn't want to talk, she simply worked alongside me. If I did want to talk, she delicately layered on the advice.

Despite her age, her hair was only slightly greying, with the rest a golden brown that hid most of the grey strands. If I simply met Sister Kristen on the street I would have thought she was in her forties. Although, the one time I brought Maggie to Sister Kristen's Home for Furry Animals, she came across a driver's license that added thirty years to my forty-something.

"No friend this time?" she inquired, looking around me toward the doorway.

"No, I think Maggie's about done with this place after the last incident. I didn't mention our strange falling out, or how I had no idea what was wrong between the two of us."

"That was almost a year ago. I'm sure Maggie's over it by now. It was only a little nip to the skin. I don't even think the teeth left a scratch."

They really hadn't left a scratch. Maggie was playing with a dog she was told she shouldn't, as it had come from an abusive family and was still impulsive. If you talked to Maggie though, the dog gave her rabies and nearly took her arm off. She equated the pain to a soldier who loses an arm and can still sometimes feel his arm itching. As you may have guessed, my friend Maggie is a drama queen. She could turn any mole hill into a mountain.

I doubted Maggie would be back anytime soon. She was not someone to forgive easily, even an abused animal.

I could feel Sister Kristen's eyes probing my gestures for signs of a problem. Whether she saw something or not, she didn't say anything. "Well, regardless, I'm glad to see you back here. In fact, I have the perfect place for you to start." She finished scribbling her name on a piece of paper and then stood up. "He's just out back. A new arrival."

"Have you heard the rumors, Sister?"

"Oh my, I don't mind rumors, Jaycee. I have too much else to think about. One day at a time is my motto."

We walked down the short hallway to a sliding door that opened into the large open yard, lined with kennels. Sister Kristen led me to kennel twelve where she pulled out a master key, unlocked the lock, and was met by the biggest, hairiest sheepdog I'd ever seen. In fact, I'd only seen sheep dogs on television, or in magazines. I couldn't believe how big and hairy that guy was. I instantly fell in love.

He lunged onto Sister Kristen's shoulders, "They call him Ghost," she said, as the dog licked her face, and she struggled to move her face side-to-side and avoid the lapping tongue. "Unfortunately, unlike a ghost, he likes to keep his presence well known."

Sister Kristen eventually got Ghost to drop to his four huge paws with a handful of jerky, which she tossed into the corner of his kennel.

"He needs to be bathed and brushed. As you can tell by his name, he's supposed to be white, not the color of mud. Then, you can feed him and take him for a walk. I'm not sure how he reacts to other dogs, but I imagine, if he reacts to dogs the way he does to people, then he'll get along just fine around here."

I dropped to my knees. "Oh, I love him. He's so cute."

As if knowing we were talking about him, Ghost ran up to me, a strand of jerky dangling from the side of his mouth. I threw my arms around him, welcoming a much-needed hug and some not so welcome slobber.

It took nearly three hours to bathe, dry off, brush, feed, and walk Ghost around the animal shelter. By the time I was done, Ghost looked like a new dog. He was easy to walk on a leash, and I could tell that whoever his previous owner was, they'd treated and trained him well. I almost didn't want to ask why he was in the shelter. Usually the only animals who come to Sister Kristen are ones that were dumped, left behind, or taken away from their owners by animal control officers for abuse. I can't say they all came here in as good a shape as Ghost.

"What do you mean we can't keep him?" Sister Kristen's voice could be heard through the open window of her office as Ghost and

I walked by. Sister Kristen was on the phone and went on, "A distribution center? I don't understand! They can't just waltz into our town and start picking out property they want to take. It doesn't work like that. At least it shouldn't."

I had a sinking feeling in my stomach. A feeling, it seemed, I was getting very much accustomed to. Something told me that whatever Sister Kristen was talking about had something to do with the same people trying to take my dad's store—Whalemart.

"Yes, I know the city owns the lease to the shelter, Mayor Johnson, but if you give them the land next to the mall, I will lose half the kennels here. Actually, we'll lose them all. We can't have the animals that close to those trucks. The smog alone will kill them. Not to mention the trucks coming in and out. These dogs need to live in a relaxing environment. Most of them come from broken homes, abandonment, or abuse. Our job is to protect them and get them to good homes.

"You just can't go and shut us down like this . . . Okay, okay, I understand you don't *think* you're shutting us down, but you are. Where are we going to go? What are we going to do? I can't exactly tell people we can't take animals anymore."

I lightly tugged on Ghost's leash. "C'mon, big boy, I don't think we should eavesdrop on Sister Kristen."

Like Dad's store, Sister Kristen's shelter was going to be taken away from me, and everyone else. There was nothing I could do. "It's not my business. Sister Kristen has to handle it." I muttered to myself, hoping by saying the words I would actually believe them.

It didn't work.

By the time Ghost was back in his kennel and I was locking up, Sister Kristen came out of the small building her office was housed in. It was obvious she was feigning a cheerful mood as her eyes were red-rimmed, and she seemed to force her smile.

"Are you all done?"

I nodded and handed the leash to Sister Kristen. "He's a great dog. I love him. Can't wait to see him in a couple days."

The tears fell down Sister Kristen's face faster than she could grab the tissue she had hidden in her palm. "Oh dear. I'm afraid we need to find somewhere else for Ghost and all the animals. Looks like your rumors are turning out to be true. I can't ignore them anymore."

While I'd overheard part of her phone conversation, I waited for Sister Kristen to let me know what was going on. I stood patiently waiting for her to collect herself. How had my life gone from such tranquility and normalcy, to tears, sadness, drama, and fear in such a short period of time? Should I tell her about my idea to find out the true owner of the mall and surrounding land?

"Thank you for your help today, Jaycee. I really do appreciate you."

She came up to me, and as if saying goodbye to a loved one going off on a long trip, she gave me a great big hug. I hugged her back, letting a tear fall from my eye and drip onto Sister Kristen's shoulder.

I tried to make sense of everything. "Where is Ghost going to go?" I whispered.

"I'm not sure yet, Jaycee. We just don't have the amenities and resources to keep him here."

Sister Kristen released me from her hug and wiped her eyes clean.

"It'll be okay. We'll figure something out. Don't worry, honey, you're still recovering yourself. Don't take on my problems."

I took a step forward and half-heartedly raised my hand to say something before I thought better of it and stopped. What could I say? Nobody listens to a kid when it comes to business. Maybe they should, but they don't. Whoever the owner was, they were willing to turn their backs on the good people of Serenity. They cared only about money and profit, not people.

"It'll be okay, Jaycee. I'll figure something out. Why don't you go on home? I hear you have a big party tonight."

Sister Kristen began walking back toward her office, her head down, shoulders slumped. She looked drained and exhausted.

"No, they won't. We need to do . . . Sister Kristen!"

Sister Kristen turned around and faced me. "Yes?"

"I'll take him! I'll take Ghost home with me!"

The faintest of smile lifted the corners of her mouth. Then she struck a curious pose. "Are you sure your parents will let you?"

"Yes, yes! They will. We've been talking about getting a dog anyway. They've been promising for years, we just haven't found the right one."

It was a lie, of course, but only a little white lie, but I was sure I could convince my parents it would be okay. A small white lie in exchange for a big white dog. What could go wrong?

"One of your parents are going to have to come by to fill out the paperwork." She paused a moment. "But, honey, I don't think it would be too much of a problem if you wanted to take him home for a couple days so your parents could get used to him. He is a little . . . *spirited*."

I could hardly stand it. I ran back to the kennel shouting "thank you" over and over to Sister Kristen. I unlocked the kennel and grabbed two handfuls of rambunctious sheepdog fur. "You're coming home with me, boy. We'll be the best of friends!"

I never even asked how he came to be in the shelter.

I can't exactly tell you my parents were thrilled with the idea of me bringing a giant white sheepdog home with me. Especially when I told them that Ghost was now a permanent resident of the family.

"We can't afford it," Mom said, "Especially not right now. You heard what might happen to the store. It will cost a fortune to feed such a huge dog, Jaycee. It's not practical."

"I know, Mom, but I can get a job. I can take care of him. You won't have to do anything."

Dad laughed at me. "I wonder how many kids a day make that same promise to their parents. We understand you want Ghost, but he's a big, and I mean a *big*, responsibility. I don't know if you would even be able to afford the food with a part-time job."

"I have money. I've been saving up. Christmas, birthday, odd jobs, I put it all aside. I never buy anything. You know that."

My parents had a mixed degree of both shock and pride as I laid out my terms. I thought I would toss some whipped cream on their hot cocoa. "I have at least a thousand dollars saved. Probably more.

It's been awhile since I counted it. Plus, Jaime has a dog house in their backyard they don't use anymore."

Jaime was a good friend of mine, and our party would be at his house later that night. I was sure he would let me have his dog house. He built it himself in hopes that his hard work would pay off in the form of his parents buying him a dog. But, they never did, so now, he used it as his personal little library. One he hadn't read in for the past two summers.

"Ah," Dad said, with an exasperated sigh.

"Don't you give in to her, Joe." Mom nudged Dad in the side. "I need some solidarity here. You're supposed to be the strong one. Without you, I'll collapse."

Dad silently nodded his head. "Well, then I guess Ghost stays. I don't have a problem if you can pay to keep him, and your mom is a weakling. So, I don't see how the answer will be no."

"Oh, my God! Are you serious? You'll let me keep Ghost!"

I couldn't exactly hide my excitement. I ran right past my parents and to Ghost who I had tied to a tree near the front door. He was sitting on his haunches licking droplets of water from a nearby bush and eagerly watching the white squirrel as it taunted him then scurried up a tree just beyond the reach of Ghost's leash. He jumped on me as soon as I closed the door.

"You're staying with us, Ghost! This is your new home. You will love it here, big guy!"

I gave him a hug and untied his leash from the tree.

"Let's go in back, and I'll show you your new home."

Our back yard was big. I knew the perfect place to put Jaime's doghouse. After a quick call to him, he was ready to get rid of the doghouse as eagerly as I was to get it. Within an hour, Jaime and his grandfather—we called him Grandpa Bear—were at our house. Dad helped them carry the doghouse into the backyard, and even before it was settled on the ground, Ghost had jumped into it, circled around inside, and lay down.

Grandpa Bear was a tall and broad-shouldered man. His skin was dark and as taut as when he was a young man. His hair was tied back in braids down to his lower back, and adorned with a single eagle feather where the braid began. A small leather bag was attached to his belt. I'd always wondered what he carried in it, expecting the items to be mystical and special. But Jaime ruined that thought by telling me he only kept tobacco and a pipe in the bag. I always felt as if he gave off an air of dignity and pride. He spoke in a slow and methodical way, as if every word was being processed for accuracy before it left his mouth. His voice was deep and seemed to come from way down in his chest. "Ghost is a good dog. He will protect you, and be loyal. He is bound by the Pact of the Fire."

Jaime whispered in my ear, "Are you ready for a story then?"

"I like your grandfather's stories. I plan to listen to a lot of them tonight."

"I'm sure he'd be happy to entertain."

Grandpa Bear walked over to Ghost and placed his strong hand on the dog's head, gently comforting Ghost. "Yes. I can sense he will be a good companion for you. Jaycee, do you know the story of the pact that First Man and First Woman made by the fire?"

I did not. "No," I said, feeling goose bumps tickling my skin. "Will you tell me?"

No one ever had to prompt Grandpa Bear to tell an ancient Lakota Sioux myth. He seemed to have thousands of them stored and as ready to be released as water from a cracked dam. You could sense the energy of the stories tumbling around inside him, waiting to be released.

"When the world was created," he went on, taking a rest on a nearby chair. "First Man and First Woman struggled to stay alive and warm through the first winter. First Dog struggled also. Deep into the winter, First Dog gave birth to her pups. Each night, she huddled in the brush of the forest, longingly watching the fire, which kept First Man and First Woman warm. First winter was severe, so cold that First Dog dared not leave her pups to search for food to fill her own belly, fearing that her pups would freeze to death in her absence. She curled around them, but the wind was bitter. Her belly shrank with hunger, and soon, she had no milk. The smallest pup perished, and First Dog felt her own life draining away as she struggled to care for the remaining pups. Fearing for the fate of the others, she knew she had no choice but to approach the fire and ask First Woman and First Man to share their food and the fire's warmth."

"Slowly, she crept to the fire and spoke to First Woman who was heavy with child. 'I am a mother,' said First Dog, 'and soon you will be a mother too. I want my little ones to survive, just as you will want your little one to survive. So, I will ask you to make a pact.' First Woman and First Man listened. 'I am about to die. Take my pups. You will raise them and call them Dog. They will be your guardians. They will alert you to danger, keep you warm, guard your camp, and even lay down their life to protect your life and the lives of your children. They will be companions to you and all your generations, never leaving your side, as long as mankind shall survive. In return, you will share your food and the warmth of your fire. You will treat my children with love and kindness, and tend to them if they become ill, just as if they were born from your own belly. And if they are in pain, you will take a sharp knife to their throat, and end their misery. In exchange for this, you will have the loyalty of my children and all their offspring until the end of time.'"

"First Man and First Woman agreed. First Dog went to her nest in the brush, and with the last of her strength, one by one, she brought her pups to the fire. As she did so, First Woman gave birth to First Child, wrapped her in rabbit skins, and nestled First Child among the pups by the fireside. First Dog lay down by the fire, licked her pups, then walked away to die under the stars. Before she disappeared into the darkness, she turned and spoke once more to First Man, 'My children will honor this pact for all generations. But if Man breaks this pact, if you or your children's children deny even one dog food, warmth, a kind word or a merciful end, your generations will be plagued with war, hunger and disease, and so this shall remain until the pact is honored again by all Mankind.' With this, First Dog disappeared into the night, and her spirit returned to the Creator.'"

I sat there speechless, mesmerized, as if I could feel First Dog in the breeze now blowing upon us.

Grandpa Bear then humbly walked away toward the truck. He turned back to Jaime. "There is much to do today. We should get home."

"Thank you," I yelled out to him. Jaime smiled back at me, but Grandpa Bear did not respond.

It was simply his way.

Chapter 10

Grandfather, Great Spirit, once more behold me
on earth and lean to hear my feeble voice.

—Black Elk

I had never felt an earthquake before, but as I brought Ghost a bowl of food and another with water, the ground started to shake. The weird feeling only lasted a few seconds, but before the movement was over, my dad was running out the back door of our house yelling, "Jaycee, Jaycee, are you okay?"

He scrambled out the door and raced in my direction.

"What was that?" I frantically cried out.

"I don't know. It felt like an earthquake. I've just never . . ."

I know what he was going to say. He'd never felt one in Serenity before. Dad was from Northern California and had experienced earthquakes growing up. But, here? Never.

Dad was a strong man, and it was rare for me to ever see him scared and not in control. The last couple of days, I'd had the opportunity to see both. And it was not a good feeling.

"A lot of weird stuff is going on here lately, Dad."

Like disappearing pills and white squirrels.

He looked around, worry on his face, and I could practically feel what he was thinking. Something in the way he held me and pulled me closer to him told me that he thought a lot of strange things were going on too. And, more than him possibly losing the store and the earthquake we'd just felt. Was there a "white squirrel" type mystery going on in his life? Something I couldn't see? After all, strange things had happened in my parents' lives. They had told me many times the story of how I was born at a highway rest area on Christmas Eve.

They always teased me that my love for chips and sodas was a direct result of being born between two big red vending machines. So, it wouldn't have surprised me to learn that they had more secrets.

"I'm fine, Dad," I reassured him, even though I didn't let go of his arm.

"Yeah, yeah. I'm sure it was just a little tremor. Not sure what caused it though. It's not like we sit on a fault line or anything. At least I don't think we do."

Mom called from inside the house, "You guys okay out there?"

Dad yelled back, "Yep. We're doing fine."

"I'm going to check on your mom. You should probably start getting ready for the party."

I nodded. I wasn't even sure I really wanted to go. In fact, if I didn't know Grandpa Bear would be there I don't think I would have gone at all.

I know Johnny wasn't interested in going to the party, but I thought about calling him just to see if he'd go with me. I still didn't know why Maggie was upset with me, but if she continued to act the way she was, I could see the party as being uncomfortable without Johnny. I needed an ally.

I've been wracking my brains since the day Maggie walked off the field, and I haven't been able to figure out what it was that was bothering her. There had been so much to think about. Our quiet little town was turning into a bee hive of natural disasters, drama, trauma, and intrigue. Naturally, Maggie would be at the center of it all.

I found that Ghost was already fast asleep in his doghouse. The tremor hardly seemed to affect him. I knelt and gave him a great big hug.

"I love you, boy. I'm so glad you're going to be a part of our family."

I followed his smile and gaze as he lifted his head and watched that little white squirrel scurry across the yard. It was probably terrified with the earthquake. "Poor little guy," I whispered to Ghost.

I brushed my hand through Ghost's thick coat of fur. "I have to run. I'll be back later tonight."

With a final kiss, I jumped up and ran inside to get dressed for the party.

Jaime greeted me at the door. I asked him two questions right off the bat: "Did Johnny show up? And where is Grandpa Bear?"

He had the same answer for both. "In the back room. Grandpa is, surprise, surprise . . . sharing some stories with a couple of people. You know. *His* way."

"Well, then you know where I'll be," I told him, and went to walk away.

"Hey, wait!" He grabbed my arm. "Maggie's here. I think you two should talk."

"I don't know why. She hasn't said a word to me since the other day. I doubt she has anything to say to me now."

"Please?"

He was practically begging me to talk to Maggie. I couldn't believe how long this had all dragged out and with me incoherent as to what the problem even was. Frankly, I just wanted Maggie to deal with it all on her own. I was tired of always being the good guy. Whatever she was mad about was her deal and not mine.

"Fine! Whatever. I didn't even do anything wrong. Where is she?"

"Sitting by Johnny in the back room listening to Grandpa Bear."

"That's an odd place for her to be."

"Yeah, well, why do you think I want you to talk to her? Something is up."

"Well, thanks for the warning anyway."

I headed straight to the den at the back of the house and sat down between Maggie and Johnny. I was sandwiched between my two best friends, and I couldn't have felt more uncomfortable. Maggie didn't even look at me when I sat down. I might as well have been invisible. Johnny scooted over to give me more room and nodded. Smiling wasn't his thing, but at least he acknowledged I was there.

Grandpa Bear was sitting on the floor in front of the group. For an old man, he was still limber and his legs were crossed, his back ramrod straight. He had apparently just finished with a story I regretted missing.

Johnny asked him, "How do you know when you need to go on a vision quest?"

But before Grandpa Bear could answer, Jacob Rogers chimed in. I like Jacob. He is funny and nice, maybe a little too goofy, but I still like him, except when he knows everything about everything, which seems like all the time.

"A vision quest, *Hembleciya*," he seemed to reiterate, although I had obviously missed the story. "You go when you're called," he replied, confident in his answer. "The Native American gods will call you and then you go. They want to test you and make sure you are devoted to them. Everyone knows that, Johnny."

Johnny pondered this for a moment, and Grandpa Bear said nothing. "That sounds more like a Christian God to test devotion, Jacob Rogers. Grandpa Bear is not Christian, Jacob Rogers."

"They're all the same. All religions are the same."

You gotta give it to Jacob. He is always very sure of his opinions. He picks a lane and stays in it.

With that declaration, Grandpa Bear raised his great paw, a hand as large as a bear's, and began to speak. "Hembleciya is to provide enlightenment when you have a question or need a path. It is not until you relieve your body of all things—food, water, toxins, thoughts, memories—that you can begin to see what the Spirit is trying to tell you. Successful, it will connect you to your Spirit Guide."

It was Maggie's turn to chime in, "Well, there are some people here who probably need to go on a vision quest, or Ham-bakey, whatever you call it." She smirked and rolled her eyes in my direction. "You know, so they can see what they do to other people."

She stood up and bumped against me as she walked out of the room, obviously in no mood to talk.

Grandpa Bear didn't react.

"How do you go on one of those he . . . he . . . hem thingies?" I asked, stammering over the unfamiliar word.

"The quest is not to be taken lightly. It is a powerful tool and answers not always answers you desire, nor are they always the answers to questions you ask. Your Spirit Guide has better understanding of the questions you need to ask, and not the questions you want to ask. For these, the Spirit Guide will help you find your path. I will tell you what Black Elk told me when I had seen fewer than this many sun dances."

He held up all ten fingers, put them down, and added two.

Jacob chimed in with his know-it-all tone, "That's less than fifteen years old. You see, there was a sun dance once a year in the middle of summer."

Grandpa Bear did not comment on Jacob's interruption. He simply went on, "I had seen fewer than fifteen sun dances when Black Elk told me his story. Shortly after I would go on my first Hembleciya, and Black Elk would not live beyond that year's harvest."

We all sat forward as if prompted to do so by spirits surrounding us. I could feel a warmth in the air and a strange dimming of lights. My head began to sway as if my vertigo from the past week was returning. However, instead of pain, I felt only comfort.

Grandpa Bear went on with what Black Elk had told him as a child. His eyes closed, and his voice slowly uttered a language I did not understand, as if he were praying, or perhaps summoning the spirit of Black Elk. Strangely, Grandpa Bear took on an unfamiliar voice as he began, "A Hembleciya is an experience of deeper understanding of nature and spirit. It is a ceremony practiced by American Indians.

"To prepare for this insight, one must first cleanse the body and mind by going through Inipi, or what most call a sweat lodge. Then with the help of a Holy Man, is told certain things and must go to a spot, usually on a holy mountain, and stay for two or three days. During this time, no food is eaten, and one does not sleep, but spends the time in deep prayer and observation."

"Many times, but not always, there is a vision. This vision is then shared with the Holy Man to help learn of its meaning. Sometimes, the meaning is not understood for several years afterward. This is part of a vision quest I was told to share with all who may be interested.

"Once, I went to pray at the top of the sacred mountain of my ancestors. As I climbed to the top, I heard voices singing as the wind blew the leaves. At the top I saw, made from many stones, a large circle with a cross inside. A medicine wheel. I knew from my teachings that this represented the circle of life and the four directions. I sat down by the edge of this circle to pray. I thought this was only a symbol of the universe."

"True," a very soft seemingly disembodied voice said. "Look and you will see the center of the Universe. Look at every created thing."

As I looked around, I saw that every created thing had a thread of smoke or light going from it.

The voice then whispered, "This cord that every created thing has is what connects it to the Creator. Without this cord, it would not exist."

As I watched, I saw that all these threads, coming from everything, went to the center of the circle where the four directions were one place (the center of the cross). I saw that all these threads were tied together or joined here at this spot.

The voice spoke again, "This is the center of the Universe. The place where all things join together and all things become one. The place where everything begins and ends. The place inside everything created."

That's when I understood that all of creation, the seen and the unseen, was all related.

The voice spoke one last time, "Yes, now you know the center of the universe. I pray to the four directions . . . hear me.

"I pray to the West which gives us rest and reflection."

"I thank you for these gifts, for without them we could not live."

"I pray to the North which gives us patience and purity."

"I thank you for these gifts, for without them we could not live."

"I pray to the East which gives us energy and emotions."

"I thank you for these gifts, for without them we could not live."

"I pray to the South which gives us discipline and direction."

"I thank you for these gifts, for without them we could not live."

"Grandmother, share with me your wisdom, and I thank you for this gift."

"Grandfather, share with me your strength, and I thank you for this gift."

When Grandpa Bear was done speaking, we all sat in silence, awed by the man and his story. In many ways, maybe Maggie was right, and I needed to go on a vision quest. It may, after all, help me figure out the problems I was facing and find a way through them.

Grandpa Bear stood up and walked away. Before he walked out of the door, he turned back toward me and looked into my eyes as if he were speaking, and I had lost my hearing. I struggled to hear and understand his unspoken words. It took me some time, but in those few seconds, I knew what he was saying. He was telling me the exact same thing that his grandson, Jaime, had told me. I needed to find Maggie.

I jumped up from the couch and ran out of the room.

As much as I searched for Maggie, I couldn't find her anywhere. No one had seen her. Even Jaime, who at times I would have thought was her stalker, had lost sight of her after she stormed out of the room when the rest of us were listening to Grandpa Bear.

By the time I'd gone outside to see if she was in her car, it was gone. Maggie had taken off from the party. Again, for something I'd done? I didn't know what I should do. Maggie was gone. I would probably have a better time at the party now knowing Maggie wouldn't be wandering around sulking, or avoiding me. Yet, at the same time, something was majorly wrong, and I needed to find out what it was. Maggie would hold it in forever and internalize her problems. She would find reasons to be mad at me, and eventually, she would twist her anger into a fist of hate directed at me. Why? I had no idea.

I'd seen her do it before. Even with our friend, Judith, she had some small problem that grew into hate. Maggie seriously didn't like Judith, and there was no real explanation for it. If anything, Judith and Maggie had more in common than any other two people in school. They were both spoiled by parents who loved them, but didn't know how to appreciate them. They were both popular and shared a love for gadgets and tech. I actually had little in common with either of them. However, growing up, Judith and I were best friends, and since fifth grade, Maggie and I were best friends. In reality, Maggie and Judith should have been best friends, and I should have been best friend to neither.

I glanced back at Jaime's house, and when I did, I was startled to see Grandpa Bear looking out through a small side window, staring straight at me. It was the same intense look he'd given me earlier.

He seemed to be silently telling me to go and find Maggie.

I listened.

Chapter 11

In order to carry a positive action, we must
develop here a positive vision.

—Dalai Lama

Despite the fact that her new sports car had come to a stop butt end jutting up toward the street, and Maggie struggled to keep her chest off the steering wheel, she still didn't bother to remove the ear buds from her ears. The thumping of the bass kept her head in a slight nod as tears rolled down her face. She'd done it again. Messed up. She managed to drop her phone on the passenger seat, then watched helplessly as it slid off the seat and bounced onto the floor mat.

Luckily, I decided to stubbornly look for her, or who knows what would have happened, or how long Maggie would have been strapped there. I didn't know what happened, but I could sure speculate. As I dialed Maggie's mother, I could feel the dread stiffening my stomach as I knew Maggie would hate me for it. She would call me a snitch, a narc, or whatever term came to her mind to say I had betrayed her. Maggie would ignore the fact that there was no way to hide the fact that she had crashed her car. As I came up on her Corvette, I could see the entire front end was destroyed. Even if we could have gotten it out of the ditch intact, we couldn't have fixed it without her parents knowing. In a small town like Serenity, everyone knows everyone, and few stories remain a secret for long. Even bank tellers know who deposits what and when, therefore their spouses know, and soon everyone is gossiping about how wealthy or poor the Joneses are.

A trickle of blood oozed down Maggie's forehead where she had struck the steering wheel. I could smell the smoky wisp of whiskey on her breath as I walked up. The still night air was not going to aid her in hiding the fact that she'd been drinking. I guess I knew the culprit. The small joint near the foot pedal told me what else was going on. My fault too? Probably would be, in Maggie's mind anyway.

Maggie was in a fit of tears, and openly sobbing.

"Stupid. Stupid. Stupid," she shouted. "How could I have been so stupid!"

"That's what I was wondering," I said, startling Maggie as I walked up.

Was it a hint of joy that I was the one who'd found her and not someone else? Or, was Maggie just too drunk and high to forget she was mad at me for some unknown slight? I'd guess the latter.

The night was quiet and the sky clear, as above us and shining brightly, I recognized my favorite constellation of Orion. It was quiet enough to hear the soft rustling of the surrounding trees, and the occasional bird speak of whistles and chirps. Orion seemed to speak to me with clarity, and I knew that I had not happened upon Maggie by chance. Something had set us on this path together, and something had pushed me to find Maggie. The hot car engine began to cool, and I could hear it pop and crackle like breakfast cereal.

Maggie was suspended in a forward posture against her seatbelt, the mascara around her eyes now streaks of deep blue, and her hair resembling a bristled scarecrow dangling from its pole in Old Man Johnson's field. Mr. Johnson had told me once that the scarecrows were in his field as much to scare away the kids who would cut through on the way to school as it was to scare away crows; it never seemed to do either very well. I resisted the urge to snap a picture of her for posterity.

I didn't bother to hug Maggie. I only had my hand on her shoulder to let her know I was there and I would help her. "Okay, can you reach the buckle if I prop you up?" I asked Maggie, not sure about the full extent of her injuries.

I assumed by the blood she had at least a concussion. Weren't we a pair?

Maggie grunted loudly as she slid her hand to her side, then declared, "Yeah. I can get it."

"Okay, you lean your body on my shoulder, and I'm going to try and hold you up while you unbuckle. Then maybe I can get you out."

Maggie was a lot heavier than I'd thought she would be, but I guess when you're a good athlete like Maggie, you are pure muscle, instead of some of the flab I had tied around my waist and tried desperately to hide. Maggie's diet consisted of lean meats, veggies, salad, salad, salad . . . beer, whiskey, and cigarettes. It was amazing we were such good friends.

As Maggie held herself up by grabbing the steering wheel, I was able to slide the seat belt around her until it was completely off. With a little flexibility, Maggie slid herself over to the seat next to her, reached down, and plucked the phone off the floor. Priorities.

I stepped back and opened the door.

"What are you doing?" I asked, amazed she was on her phone without knowing the full extent of her injuries.

"I need to Tweet this."

"You need to what?"

"I'm Tweeting this. Epic bad ending."

She held her phone screen up so I could see the Tweet, #stupidmoves

"At least you know it is stupid. What happened anyway?"

Maggie climbed out of her car and only then could she see how bad of a situation she was in. "Oh my God, Jaycee. What am I going to do? I can't tell my parents about this. They're going to kill me! I need your help. You need to help me get the car out of this ditch."

For the moment, Maggie forgot she was mad at me, and I didn't mind. In fact, I hoped, if she had a concussion, that she would forget about how upset she was with me entirely and we could get back to the way things were before. Maybe she could Tweet, #BestiesHelpBesties

"How did this happen, Maggie?" I raised my voice.

I couldn't believe this. Of all the things Maggie had done in the past, this one was possibly one of the worst. She could have been killed or seriously hurt.

"I don't know. I was driving. This new song came on. You know, the Beyoncé one."

"No, I don't know."

"Oh, that's right. You're a classical chick. Well, anyway, the song's sick. I was bouncin' in the car enjoying myself—."

"Have you been drinking?" The sharp stench of alcohol and tobacco was now more than a light scent. It engulfed us. "You told me you weren't going to drink anymore."

"Hey, don't put this on me!" Maggie stammered.

"Well, whose fault is it, Maggie? You're the one who is drunk. You're the one whose car is in the ditch. I don't see any other guilty party in the ditch with you. You're lucky you're still alive!"

"Well I am, and I'm not even hurt. So, it wasn't that bad."

"You could have been hurt though. I begged you, Maggie. I begged you not to drive drunk. You just got your license, for God's sake! You know you're going to lose it, right? If the police don't take it from you, your parents will."

Maggie stumbled forward a bit, and then caught herself. "My parents don't need to know. We can take care if this without them, right?"

She gave me her most winning, pathetic, puppy-dog-eyes look.

"Just tell me what happened."

I'm only human. I did look up to see if Orion was frowning down on me.

"That's just it. I didn't do anything wrong. You see, I was dancing in the car to Beyoncé. Suddenly, this cute little white squirrel darted out into the road and stopped right in front of me. It just stayed there facing me, watching me. So, of course, I swerved my car. But, as I did, it moved again in the direction I swerved, so I jerked my car again in the opposite direction. The next thing I knew, I was in the ditch. Then you showed up."

"A white squirrel?"

"Yeah, why?"

I thought of the very rare, unusual squirrel I've been seeing around my house. It was white too. Strange. "Nothing. It doesn't matter. You know you can't hide this from your parents. Somebody has probably already called them."

"Yes, I can. We just need to call one of the guys and have them bring their truck out here. We can tow it out, then see if any of them can repair it. They'll never know."

It's true. Several of the guys on the soccer team are car buffs. Being in northern Minnesota, most of them have trucks too. This wouldn't be a big deal for any of them, and more likely, the guys would love to play a role in hiding something like this from Maggie's parents. And coming to her rescue, sure, Maggie was right, we probably could hide this from her parents. That is . . . except for one thing . . .

Twin car lights approached and were shining on us before Maggie, or I realized it was even there. It was like we were on a stage with floodlights on us.

"Uh, Mags, I need to tell you something."

Tears began to fall from Maggie's eyes again. "Let me guess. You need to tell me that we can't hide it from my parents because you already called my parents and told them I was in an accident."

I simply nodded helplessly.

"It's all right." Maggie stumbled toward me, obviously a little more drunk than she'd thought she was. She put her arms around me. "You know, you're the only one I wanted to call, right?"

"I know."

And for some reason I did know that. Despite what was going on, I had a sense that Maggie had wanted to call me, and had been in the process of doing so when she dropped her phone on the floorboard.

"I know my parents would have found out about the car. I was just hoping to hold them off a bit. And, Jaycee . . ."

"Yes?"

"I'm sorry. It's just that . . . I need to tell you something."

I held Maggie close to me as she struggled to speak.

"Why did you make me look bad in front of the U scouts at the game?"

"Huh?"

"You made that awesome play instead of me. Why did you do that?"

"Maggie, you tripped, and I was in position to win the game. There was nothing you could have done after you tripped. It happens." I shrugged. "What else could I have done?"

Maggie began to laugh louder and louder until she was crying again. She was hysterical, and I wondered again about a concussion. The feeling was a bright memory in my own mind.

"You know? I forgot all about that I tripped." She laughed. "I just remember seeing you take the shot on goal and winning the game. That should have been my shot."

"That's why you were mad at me?"

She paused, and looked at me. "Maybe. I guess."

She had more to say, I could see. But perhaps it was her parents approaching, or she wasn't ready to tell me. But whatever it was, she didn't explain the strange look on her face.

The car stopped. It was left running as both of Maggie's parents leapt from the vehicle and ran toward us. I was surprised to see them together. Apparently, they had reconciled or something.

"Hello, Mr. and Mrs. Thorsett."

Mr. Thorsett turned to me as he passed by, distracted, and said, "Hello, Jaycee. Thank you for calling us."

Then he continued past his daughter and followed his wife to where the car was nearly vertical on its nose in the ditch. "Doesn't look like there is much damage. Well, I should say at least it can be fixed," he commented to his wife.

"No. No, it doesn't look too bad. That's good." Mrs. Thorsett finally turned to her daughter. "You're so lucky, young lady. You could have really destroyed this car. We bought it new for you. It's only a week old."

I was stunned. I could also see Maggie starting to cry again. I knew exactly what was wrong, and in a way, I felt as if I were holding back tears as well. "They care, Maggie. They really do," I whispered to her.

Mrs. Thorsett came back to us. "Is your phone broken too? We just bought that one last month after you broke your other one. I don't get you, Maggie. We buy you one thing after another. All new. All the best. And the way you repay us is to treat your stuff like garbage. I don't get it. I just don't get it."

Flashing lights were coming toward us in the distance. Maggie's mother looked up, "That'll be the tow truck. We didn't call the police."

"Jaycee, thank you again for calling us. I'm glad to see at least one of you girls has some sense in your brain. If you want to hop in the car, I'll give you a ride home."

"No thanks, Mrs. Thorsett. I can just walk. I have to pick something up on my way home anyway."

I hugged Maggie. "It'll be okay. I'll see you in school tomorrow."

Maggie nodded and dropped her face into my shoulder. I could feel the tears soaking through and put an arm around her.

"We're going to be laughing about this in a year. You just wait."

Maggie grabbed her phone and tapped it a few times, then showed her Twitter feed to me, *This sucks! #thankgodforfriends.*

I could tell there was something else Maggie wanted to share with me. I just knew there was something more going on. She just wasn't ready to share it yet.

I smiled, deciding to let Maggie take her time until she was ready to talk, and walked toward home. In the distance, the last thing I heard Maggie's mother say was, "You're lucky. If we had to buy you another car, it wouldn't be as nice as this one."

*****

Instead of going home, I went to the bluff overlooking Serenity. My parents knew I was going to be home late, and I didn't think it would bother them if I stayed out a little longer. I needed a little time on my own.

I was sitting in the woods where I had last seen the white squirrel. It was no longer there. I took out the small notebook I always carry with me. It is simple and unassuming, much like myself, which is one of the reasons I like it so much.

Then I began to write.

My Church
My processional is a flock of geese
Heading South in unity of purpose.
My church pew is a rock on a bluff,
Overlooking a mighty river
As it flows from the source to the collective.
My communion is a patch of ripened berries
Bathed in the falls' sunlight.
My prayers ride the wispy clouds,
That float on a deep blue canvas.
My church is the boundless wonder
Of nature's diversity.
My God is the creator of all that falls
Outside man's concept of what God is supposed
to be.

I love Maggie so much, but she does make life hard. Today, Maggie crashed her car. Something about seeing and trying to avoid hitting a white squirrel. But I am upset that she was driving drunk—likely the true culprit to her crash—and she'd been smoking too. I could smell it on her. I don't know why she acts like this. Oh wait, yes, I do. I could see tonight how her parents treat her. It's something I've seen many times before. They don't act like they care for her. Tonight was all about the car. They never once asked her how she was. I'm sure they were mad, but they showed no love at all, not even the slightest affection.

I feel like Maggie is my responsibility in many ways. Her parents shower her with gifts, but nothing else. Even with this crash, I'm sure they will give Maggie something extravagant as a way of trying to say, "Yeah, sure, we care." But, I never get the feeling that they do. I don't think Maggie feels the love either. And I think she tries to dull her hurt feelings with alcohol and pot.

Another note. Dad said he thinks he is going to lose the store, and I get the impression Sister Kristen feels the same about the animal rescue. Everything is crumbling, and I'm scared. Very, very scared. There's way too much change happening at once.

Well, I need to go. I'm in my special place in the woods. I'm glad my home is not like Maggie's.

Oh! One more thing for myself. I've been working on a poem to describe myself. I don't know how well it describes me, but I like it. With all that's been going on lately I think it fits. I call it "My Country Heart:"

Gucci shoes and Madison Ave blues.
She's just a city girl with country heart.
Limo rides and fashion shows,
Uptown glitz and champagne woes.
She just wants to feel the long green grass between her toes.
She has never seen a rodeo.
She has never seen a bronc bust for home.
She brushes her hair with a golden comb,
Wondering if there is another way out of this city's dome.
She buys her jeans in a limousine.
She's never heard croaking frogs sing their songs to a bubbling stream.
She's never swum free in a midnight fog.
She hears the country songs and she knows there's more,
She closes her eyes and tries to smell the mountain air.
She's just a city girl with a country heart,
Not really sure how to play her part.
Takes long walks in a gated park,
Wondering nights how to jump the fence.
Wants to run but she can't afford the rents.
She is just a city girl with a country heart.

My parents were still awake as I walked in the front door. They both came up to me and gave me a hug. The difference between my parents and Maggie's is immeasurable. I wouldn't be surprised to learn Maggie has never received a hug in her life. At least not from her parents.

Then Dad stepped back and asked, "Have you been smoking?"

"What? No . . . I would never. I just . . ."

"I can smell it on you. Are you okay? Where have you been?"

I told them the story about Maggie. "And the smell must be from Maggie. I've never smoked before and never want to."

Mom couldn't help herself. "So, Maggie's been drinking again?"

It sounded more like her question was a statement directed at me, asking if am I making wise decisions, or am I allowing Maggie to take me down with her?

I looked down at my feet trying to think of every excuse I could think of to protect Maggie. Truth was, I couldn't think of any good excuse. Yes, she was drinking again. And, yes, she was smoking again. Not just cigarettes either. She was smoking pot, and maybe more. But, all that came out of my mouth was, "Yes."

"I see," Mom replied. "And you weren't out with her tonight?"

"No. I was at Jaime's party and the bluff. Maggie was at the party for a little while, but I didn't see anyone else drinking or anything. I think it was just Maggie"

Dad put his arm on my shoulder. "Sounds like you've had a long day. I'm not sure we like you hanging out with Maggie so much, but we can talk about it tomorrow. Why don't you just head up to bed?"

He bent down to hug me, and I couldn't dismiss the slight inhale Dad made as he gently squeezed me goodnight. Mom did the same thing, and I realized, both of my parents thought I had indeed been drinking.

Apparently, my word didn't count for much. But, then again, did I smell like smoke and alcohol? It was a question I'd spend the rest of the night pondering as I twisted and turned in bed, making a balled-up knot of my bed sheets.

Something happened to me that night, and I don't know how to explain it. Maggie was on my mind along with Johnny, Dad's store, and surprisingly, an earthquake that should have never happened.

I dreamt of Grandpa Bear, and a vision quest. My vision quest.

Was I to embark on one of my own? Is that what all these signs were telling me?

Had I found my quest or reason to embark on one?

The dreams filled me throughout the night. I could feel my body drenched in sweat, and my sheets became drenched too.

If it was a vision quest I needed to embark on, I had something else to get through first. Something terrible was going to happen, and while it was occurring, I wasn't so sure I'd even live long enough to embark on a quest. I might never be able to answer my questions and bring the world that was falling apart back to being the great world I once knew. I dreamt that I was surrounded by question marks, dancing around and mocking me.

Chapter 12

A blocked path also offers guidance.

—Mason Cooley

I was choking on the air surrounding me, as if all the oxygen had been replaced by cotton balls. The thickness of my tongue collapsed back within my throat, blocking the only airway remaining allowing me to breathe. Blood was pouring from both of my nostrils. In a state of extreme panic, and without any idea what to do, I ran from my house. I found my way deep into the forest, away from cars, houses, friends, family, or anyone who could help me.

For some reason, I knew no one could help me, and I didn't want the world to see me like this—a sweaty and blood-matted image of a teenage girl who couldn't handle the pressure of being a teenager. I ran as fast as I could, not knowing exactly where I would end up, but only that I would stop when my ankles buckled, my feet tripped, and my body failed me, leaving me to die alone. My body was to be discovered days, or perhaps, weeks later.

I don't know how long I'd been unable to breathe. It seemed an eternity as I focused on one foot followed by another. The dirt path ahead of me, beaten by deer and rabbits for decades, was clear of tree roots, rocks, fallen branches, vines, and brush. I'd never seen the path so clear, yet upon my death, I could see nothing but clarity.

I knew I would collapse soon. A sharp pain, like a thin needle puncturing my chest time and again, was slowly souring each pump of my heart and the blood in my body was growing fetid with each pulse. I, of course, ran through images of vampires and zombies. What kid wouldn't? Heck, what adult wouldn't? But, I knew I hadn't been bitten, nor did I believe a zombie virus had struck me.

Something else was happening. Something all too real . . . my mind slowly began to fade into a dizzyingly confused craze. *Something all too real, or was it?*

My feet were heavy, encased in lead, as I stumbled forward. I felt the splintering of my kneecaps as they took the full weight of my upper body slamming down on legs that could no longer withstand the shock of an odd collapse and the weight, which only now lay upon me.

> Weight of the world
> Depends upon me
> It will all end
> It will all begin here
> Weight of the world
> Weight of the world.

And I truly felt that this pain, this struggle to move forward, was indeed the weight of the world being thrust upon my shoulders. I was being led . . . *no!* I was being dragged, pulled, and thrust forward like an ancient slave. This had all happened before. Not to me, but to others. I could feel them around me, these men of slavery. These men who were not slaves at all, but chose the path I was being led down.

I could hear the words of Father Paul. I considered him among my most trusted friends. In his words, I'd heard him utter to me from across his desk, "We're all given a path to follow, Jaycee. Some people find it on their own, and others are destined, sometimes dragged to their destiny whether they want to be or not. Take Noah, for example." He smiled, knowing how ridiculous the story of a man gathering two of every animal aboard a great boat was to a modern teenager. "Saving the world and repopulating humanity was hardly what he thought his destiny was. Millennia later, we still talk about him. He's a household name, almost as popular as the Kardashians."

Even I couldn't stifle a laugh with the comparison of Noah and the seemingly debased and amoral career politicians.

Then, I hadn't taken his words as directed at me. But, what did he mean? Did he know what was happening to me, what would happen to me? Certainly not. I couldn't imagine he did. He would have told me in more clear and certain terms. I'm sure he would have.

I was intensely tired as vertigo once again struck me, remembering the words of Father Paul. My eyelids dropped like heavy steel shutters. My chin hit my chest, sending another pulse of sharp pain through my heart and down to my pelvis. When I opened my eyes, I could see the blood that had splashed on my arms, as I was still being dragged along the trail.

I stopped.

It wasn't as if I had hit a wall, slowed, or even knew I would stop. I was just suddenly standing still, my arms drooped forward, my head lolling on my neck, my body weak, yet being held up like a marionette, controlled by Geppetto himself. *Call me Pinocchio, the gaunt, bloody, lifeless, and dying puppet not yet ready to accept the divine role set before me.*

As if my Geppetto had had a heart attack, my strings were let loose, and I collapsed to the ground dead—so I thought. At least that's how it felt—like a quick release from the strings of life to the nothingness of death.

Then my reality switched gears, like one movie stopping and another beginning.

I felt like a new person. My arms and sleeves were still streaked with blood, although it was dark, almost black, and dry and flaking, as if I had baked in a pottery kiln. My sweat was dry too, forming a powdery coating over my body.

But my personal assessment of my body became of much less interest when I saw the white squirrel staring at me. Its eyes were red but translucent, like deep ruby marbles, and they looked through me as if this young squirrel had known me my entire life. However, that couldn't be true, and I was almost fully aware that squirrels live less than ten years, and I was nearly eighteen. It sat there staring at me, its nose in a constant state of twitching as if the creature was tasting the air, wondering if the sour smell was coming from me. The squirrel was a magnificent white, unmarred by mud, grass, or any other debris you'd figure a forest creature would catch in its fur. The squirrel's tail was large and bushy, standing in an elegant arch above the animal's head. To be so small, he was a magnificent and elegant little guy, who made me smile.

"You would not believe me if it were not for the pain." Those words, unattached to a human voice, echoed through my head. I knew it wasn't possible, but in the same moment, I knew those words were from the squirrel, and its stare into my eyes were enough to convince me. *"Do not expect the pain to end. For you are my child, and speak upon my word. My word is the divine. Pain is only abated by the message that has come to fruition."*

I was tired and weak. My head collapsed onto the ground, and my mouth filled with grass. In a voice quite unlike my own, I told the beautiful white squirrel, "Ffff . . . off." The word was unnatural to me, and as such the words, I wanted to say would not come out, but I assumed the squirrel got the gist, as I was suddenly burning, lit on fire, and screaming as I felt the pain of demons ripping my flesh from the inside as they swarmed to escape from my every pore.

The squirrel had sat by my side throughout the ordeal. And when I recovered, I looked up to see it staring back at me. Sorrow was now in those ruby eyes, but also questioning, and filled with curiosity about me.

Is she the one? I hope she is strong enough. Again, they were disembodied words that I assumed were coming from the squirrel.

I don't know if I was supposed to hear those words, or thoughts, but as soon as I blinked I found myself awake at the bottom of the stairs in our house. My dad was holding my hand, and my mother was crying. I realized my head was lying in a pool of sticky iron-smelling blood. Strangely, I thought, *Is that smell going to come out of my hair? Gross!*

"The ambulance will be here shortly, Joe. Oh god! What in the world happened? Oh god, please, please, please don't take my little girl."

Dad's hands were strong, a sure sign of someone who'd spent the better part of his life with a hammer and wrench in them. He held my hand gently though, his other hand on my shoulder. "It'll be okay, Jaycee. I think you musta fell down the stairs. Don't move. We have the paramedics coming."

I fell? But, I didn't fall. I was in the forest. I was running. I was dying. There was a squirrel, and it was . . . beautiful. It talked to me, right?

I woke up in a hospital bed. This was getting to be a habit. A bad one. The dull drone of some nearby machine seemed to be giving me as much of a headache as the vomiting had earlier. A soft *beep . . . beep . . . beep . . .* was not too far off.

"Dad?" I croaked weakly, my throat dry. I could hardly hear the word come out myself. I couldn't turn my head. Well, at least I couldn't turn it easily. "Dad?" I repeated.

"I'm here, honey. Don't worry. The doctor said you're going to be just fine."

He came up to my bed and held my hand. I could feel the uncomfortable movement of something under my forearm. It felt like a small snake sliding under my skin, hibernating and not willing to move.

My dad must have realized my puzzlement. "It's something to take blood. They said it was better than pricking you a lot. Just stay still, Jaycee. It's gonna be okay."

"I don't understand," I said. "What happened?"

"Well, we don't know for sure. Your mom and I thought you had—"

I could hear the choking sobs of my mom in the background, stopping Dad from continuing.

"Well, the doctor thinks you were just dehydrated. Between soccer, how hot it's been lately, and then your frolicking in the woods, you were just dehydrated."

"Dehydrated," I said, pondering what I remembered. I guess that would explain it. The only thing I remembered was vomiting and talking to a . . . oh my god! Was I talking to a squirrel? Or, more curious, was a squirrel talking to me? The doctor was right. I was dehydrated. That sometimes led to hallucinations—a pretty big one at that.

Mom came over from where she'd been sitting. Her eyes were red, but lately that's how they'd always been. It was like she was indebted to perpetually cry. She hadn't been like that even a few months ago when she'd wake me up with a smile in the morning and would greet me with a wider smile in the afternoon when I got home from school. I don't know if she was sad these days because I'd be graduating high school in a few months and then going off to college, or if it was something else.

Neither of my parents were happy about the incident with Maggie the night before, and I couldn't help but wonder if they were internally punishing me for my association with Maggie. But, they loved Maggie, right? Or, did they? Either way, I didn't like seeing Mom like this. It just wasn't like her.

"Your dad found you on the stairs covered in blood, Jaycee. We were so scared, baby. But, you're fine now. You just need to relax for a few days, and drink a lot of liquids."

She slid her hand along my forehead, brushing the hair out of my eyes as she used to do when I was a little kid. Jeez, if I didn't know any better I'd have thought there was much more going on than me simply passing out and hitting my head on the stairs.

"Maggie stopped by," she went on, "you were sleeping, so she said she would just see you at home. She brought that by."

Mom's hand pointed to a signed soccer ball in a chair. It looked like the whole team, and a couple random people had signed the ball. Although it was the big purple letters in all caps that said, "GET BETTER, LOSER," along with the unintelligible signature, I noticed first. That was Maggie's. I smiled as I recognized the signatures of my twelve best friends. No matter what happened, and how tough things got, they always seemed to be behind or beside me.

"How long do I have to stay here, Mom?"

Doctor Billingsley's voice was the first to speak up as he walked into the room just as I finished asking. "I'd say you can go home whenever you feel like it. You're doing fine, and I don't see any need for you to stay any longer than you want. Just eat, drink a lot of water in this heat, and take care of yourself."

If he said anything else, I didn't catch it, as I seemed to be hallucinating again. That same white squirrel, with deep crystalline eyes, was sitting outside on the window ledge staring in at me.

If I didn't know any better, which apparently I didn't, I'd say it looked as though the squirrel was trying to figure out how to pop open the acorn in its tiny hands. As if it had never seen one before.

I looked at my parents. They weren't noticing the squirrel. I was exhausted, and my body ached, but there was only one thing on my mind. "I think we better get out of here. I'm pretty sure I'm going crazy."

They both gave a lighthearted chuckle, and glanced up to the window, curious, as if they saw nothing at all.

*****

I never understood why Maggie hated staying home from school. I would think it was the opposite. But, she insisted that staying home from school was one of the most miserable things that could happen to her during the year. Don't think for a minute she was talking about classes either. Maggie needed to have people around her. She had to be a part of the social scene, even better if she was the center of attention. Missing even the smallest of rumors or gossip would have practically killed her. It's funny. Maggie hated classes and learning, but couldn't imagine being out of school at any cost. I loved classes and learning, but relished the days I could be alone. So in spite of being best friends, we were opposites in that way. Being alone for me was a time to reflect. I could write, and oh how I love writing. Glancing over at my bookshelf, I could see dozens of unique notebooks I'd used the last few years to record some of my inner-most thoughts. I have books of poetry and journals recording my diary notes. Other books are filled with sketches of nearly anything in nature I could sketch. There were flowers, birds, a view of Serenity from the bluff, and by the end of the day, there will be a curious white squirrel, with red eyes, who doesn't know how to crack open a nut.

I walked over to my bookshelf, scanned the books, and grabbed a small leather writing journal with the image of a rose burnt into the cover, like a cattle brand, and a sketch book; it was much more simple with a red hard cover. From the top shelf, I pulled out my pencil case, and then walked back to my bed. I was already feeling a lot better. Aside from the small cuts on my face, and lack of make-up—I wear very little of anyway—I was starting to look normal again. I plopped down on the bed and curled up against the wall where I could look out the window at our backyard and the woods behind us.

It took me nearly an hour to sketch that squirrel from memory. As strange as it sounds, I was hoping to see it show up in my back yard. But, I knew better. I'd never seen a white squirrel before in my life. What was the chance I would see it at the bluff, outside my hospital room, and then again in my back yard? It would be astoundingly impossible.

It has been a week since Dad told us that he thought he was going to have to close his store down. He didn't say much to me, but I could tell by my mom's crying and slumped shoulders that it would be coming soon, and they didn't have any plans on what to do next. Maybe it was good that all this happened. I can only say that my condition seems more of a mental breakdown than a bout of dehydration. I was talking to a squirrel, for god's sake!

Anyway, I've only caught bits and pieces of what has been going on around town, but it just seems like this huge, giant store named Whalemart was about to swamp our town and kill off all the small fish, like my wonderful stepdad. What's worse is that no one is doing anything to stop them. So, Dad thinks his time for owning his own business is coming to a close. Going out with a whimper. No one seems to have any ideas about stopping the big whale from swallowing all the small fish in town. We were all gonna be swallowed up like Jonah that I'd learned about in literature class. The mental image of the mayor pocketing an envelope kept flashing in my mind, and each time it did, I got a sick feeling in the pit of my stomach. Were my parents, Sister Kristen, and all the others in the strip mall being sold out for greed? It was hard to fathom.

I feel desperate to help, to do something. But what am I to do? I'm a seventeen-year-old girl who graduates high school in a few months. I'll be out of here soon. But then what? What about my parents? And now I have another life—Ghost—to be responsible for.

I put the pencil down and glanced at the sketch of the squirrel. I wasn't sure how I would capture the white in a pencil sketch, but strangely, the image was almost identical to that of the squirrel I'd seen earlier. I looked down on the sketchpad, smiled, and had no clue how I'd suddenly become such a great illustrator.

"What up, brat!"

Maggie's presence shocked me more than anything. I glanced at the clock across the room. It wasn't even noon yet. I asked her, "Aren't you supposed to be in school?"

"I skipped, yo."

Her fingers were in a flurry as she tapped away a text to someone. Then she looked back up at me. "There wasn't anything much going on at school. I'd heard all the gossip I needed for a week. Did you know Brendan and Sissy were a thing?"

I shook my head, no. How would I know that? I barely knew when Maggie was "dating" someone. One day, she was madly in love with Joshua, the next . . .

She didn't stop to see if I'd known or not. "Oh! And that kennel you work at—"

"Sister Kristen's Creature Comforts," I quickly corrected her.

"Yeah, yeah, whatever. That place. Word has it they're shutting down soon."

"What? Where did you hear that?"

Maggie looked around as if someone could be nearby, then she leaned in closer to me, and whispered, "Okay, well, not a reliable source. Let's just say this Whalemart thing has crossed a bridge and is heading this way."

"So, basically you don't know anything about it."

Five minutes rolled by as Maggie anxiously went on about who was dating who after the weekend, how Mr. Krill's toupee kept falling off in algebra, and how the crap they serve the school for lunch is getting worse. The only thing that stopped Maggie was the ding of her phone, as whomever she was texting responded back. I waited while Maggie finished texting and then tapped my hand on the bed.

"Come on. Put that thing down and sit. You need a little rest from technology."

We both laughed, knowing that would never happen.

"So, you doing all right then? Everyone's been asking about you. Rumor is you went crazy and started punching yourself in the face."

"Of course." I couldn't help but laugh at the ridiculousness. "I just . . . well, I don't know for sure what happened. The doctor said it was dehydration."

"What? That's crazy. You drink more water than anyone else I can think of, and it's not like you put that much effort into soccer practice."

I slapped her shoulder and joked, "Get out of here. I am *dying*, and this is how you treat me?"

Maggie slapped me on the leg.

"Seriously though. We were worried, Jaycee. We didn't know what happened. I got a text from Joe saying you were being rushed to the hospital. He didn't reply after that, so I ran over. You looked sick, girl. And not good sick, but you looked like crap."

"Well, I feel better. So, we don't need to go on about it."

"Yeah, I guess." Maggie slid over closer to me, lying down on the bed. "You'll have to deal with all of that when you get back to school."

I don't know what was weirder: the fact that Maggie hadn't picked her phone up when another text came through, or that Maggie was actually listening to something I said. But, when I saw her swipe her fist against a cheek, and tears began to fall from her eyes, I realized that seeing her cry was the weirdest thing I'd ever seen Maggie do in the ten years we'd been best friends. She looked at me and then buried her nose deep into the pillow between me and my bed, hiding her face like an ostrich turning eggs in the sand.

Her voice was muffled at first and I couldn't make any of it out.

"What'd you say, Mags?"

Again, she talked into the pillow, rather than to me, and I couldn't hear her. Her chest was heaving, and I wondered if what I'd had earlier was contagious, but I'd soon find out how wrong that thought was.

Maggie lifted her face from the bed, but still didn't meet my eyes. "I said, I think I'm pregnant."

It was as if I were watching a movie. "How's that even possible? I mean, you are still a . . . Maggie, You're a virgin! How can you be pregnant?"

Maggie's cheeks were flushed, and the tears never slowed. She looked at me, biting her lower lip, and then dropped her eyes.

*****

When my world fell apart that day, I realized how little *my* world mattered to that of someone else. Maggie may be pregnant, or at least she thinks she is. Will her downward spiral ever end? Will she take me down with her?

There was only one thing I could think of, and it kept circling around in my head like a vulture hovering above road kill. Whatever this feeling was, it wouldn't go away. *I need to talk to Grandpa Bear. I need his wisdom and his help. This is too much for me.*

I glanced toward my nightstand where I'd once had a bottle of pills supposed to help me ignore the pain from my concussion. I never took them, and they went missing before I dared to try a pill solution. Now, however, I wished I had them. If anything, they could take me from the mood I was in.

Maybe they would have been good for my hallucination. Although, something told me that Grandpa Bear was already preparing everything I needed. I had never put it together before, but the holy man he talked about—using English terminology I know the Lakota would have never used—was none other than himself. Grandpa Bear, descendant of Crazy Horse, descendant of Black Elk, was no one other than the holy man his people talked about on their vision quests.

He would help me go on a quest of my own, and when done, I hoped he could share with me the answers I desperately seek. Most of all, I hoped he would be able to tell me what my quest meant . . . and soon. Although, I suppose it was my spirit guide who would be the one to answer that.

Soccer, school, the animal shelter, my dad's business, and my best friend's problems would all have to wait for me to discover my purpose and my future. Or if I even had one.

But the moment I thought I had figured out a pathway, the universe had another idea.

Chapter 13

FIRE!

For what shall it profit a man, if he gain the whole
world, and suffer the loss of his soul?

—Jesus Christ

Maggie and I ran. The screeching, screaming, urgent sounds of
police, fire, and ambulance vehicles drove us like cattle down the hill
and toward the center of town.

Soon, we could see billowing black smoke coming from the
area of the Catholic cathedral, St. Sebastian's, where I had been earlier meeting with Father Paul. We stopped to catch our breath and
Maggie said, "Oh, my god, Jaycee! Is the church on fire?"

"Maybe not. Maybe it's a bad car wreck or something. Let's
go see," I said, grabbing her by the hand and pulling her along the
cracked sidewalk.

It was another project the town never seemed to have the money
to fix.

My brain scrambled to sort out what I was seeing versus what
my heart was feeling. Whatever cataclysmic event was causing all the
sirens and horns, odds were, we would know somebody affected by
whatever was happening. The town was that small. Penned into a
narrow valley, we were like a family.

And so, Maggie and I ran. Down the hill, up another hill, and
finally down again and across the town square with its bronze statues
of soldiers, green space, benches, and shady oak trees. And we could
finally see the fire.

On the eastern edge of the park, we saw a group of people, among them Father Paul, wearing a house robe and slippers, his sparse hair tousled. He looked like any frightened homeowner watching his and God's house go up in flames.

The entire church complex, including the Sunday school building, and the rectory—Father Paul's home—were in flames, smoke pouring from stained glass windows that I had always thought would be there for my wedding pictures some day. It was terrifying, life-changing, and sad.

Maggie and I approached the group and Father Paul turned toward us. I could see the red rim of his eyes, his tear-stained cheeks, and the trembling hands that were normally so steady and strong.

"Father Paul," I said, "I'm so sorry. What happened? Are you okay?"

"Hi, Jaycee. We don't quite know yet what caused the fire. It seems to have started in the main sanctuary, maybe in the choir loft. The fire marshal will have to investigate."

"I'm just glad you're okay. But . . . your collections . . ."

"All gone, my dear. I have what is on my back. This ratty old bathrobe. That's about it. But I do have my faith, and that will sustain me . . . "

He broke into sobs and couldn't say anything else. It was so sad to see this man who had comforted and sustained our little town all these years, so broken.

I found a reporter I know who works at the Serenity Sentinel. "Hi, Jill. What do you know about the fire?"

"Not much, Jaycee," she said. "The fire chief said something about 'no obvious ignition point' and then he said something strange . . ."

"What," I asked, desperate to put this devastation in some sort of logical context. So many strange things had been going on, this was just a punch in the gut.

"He said something about spontaneous combustion. Sorry, that's all I got. Gotta run now and get to the paper. The editor wants at least a slug line in an hour."

Spontaneous combustion? In the church? I couldn't help but wonder if this was a direct message from God. After all, he did despise the moneychangers, and the Catholic Church had gotten more and more wealthy in the last few decades. Father Paul's immense collections were proof of assets that could have been used to do lots of things for the town. People worked hard, tithed, and never seemed to see the fruits of their charity.

As I was pondering the unthinkable, Maggie came running up to me.

"Jaycee, you'll never guess . . ."

"Mags, at this point, I'd probably believe aliens came down in a space ship and started the fire."

"I've been on Twitter and Instagram. It's all abuzz about the church catching on fire. People are saying it's a sign."

"A sign of what, Mags?"

"No one knows. But there are rumors . . ."

"Let's not start spreading rumors. Things are bad enough. I'm going to check on Sister Kristen and make sure she's okay. Things like this really upset her."

"Okay," Maggie said, sounding disappointed. "I'll stay here and keep my eyes and ears open. You got your Bat Phone?"

I felt my pocket. "Yeah, but it probably doesn't have much of a charge left on it. Gotta run."

I took off toward the other end of the park, the strip mall, and Sister Kristen's animal rescue at the southern end.

Just as I turned to leave the park, a movement above my head caught my eye. I looked up and saw a white squirrel—*the* white squirrel?—looking down at me from a low branch. Its bushy tail was pert but the critter's eyes looked sad.

A sad squirrel, Jaycee? You're losing it, girl.

Still, I couldn't help but think it was odd how this squirrel seemed to get around, from my house, to the school, and now the park. When big things were happening, he seemed to always be present. I couldn't decide if that was a bad omen, or a comforting presence.

Guess time will tell, I thought. *But I'm leaning toward the latter.*

I found Sister Kristen, unlike everyone else in town who was in the town square by now, behind the rescue center checking on her beloved animals. It had gotten dark, and she was using her big Maglite flashlight, shining it in the rabbit hutch, around in the big birdcage, and over the cat enclosure. The animals all seemed to be okay, but restless, as if their world had been rattled. Probably how they had all reacted to the earthquake. That shook us all up.

I coughed, so I wouldn't startle her. "Sister Kristen?"

She turned toward me. "Oh, hi, Jaycee. What brings you here?"

"The fire. Everyone in town is there, and there was nothing more I could do, so I wanted to make sure you and the animals are okay."

"Well, that's sweet, dear. I'm fine. Very sad, of course. So much pain recently for our little slice of heaven. At least I've always thought of Serenity as heaven on Earth. These days? Not so sure anymore."

Sister Kristen looked very sad. The acrid smell of smoke in the air didn't help. It wasn't a pleasant fall smell of burning leaves. It smelled like evil. And death. And bad things. But I wasn't about to let Sister Kristen's sudden bout of melancholy and negativism get me down. God always has a plan.

"Don't worry, Sister. Serenity will be okay. And you and I will make sure the animals are okay too, right?"

I gave her my best, most upbeat smile to try to cheer her up. And it seemed to work!

"You are absolutely, one hundred percent right, Jaycee. Let's check the rest of the critters, okay?"

We took inventory of the cages and various enclosures, like the terrarium with a garden snake, as Sister Kristen checked them off on her clipboard. Everything was present and accounted for. None of the creatures seemed worse for the bad air quality. The bunnies' noses were twitching, and that made me smile for the first time in many hours.

"Father in heaven," I whispered, "thank you for the gift of life among the devastation."

I heard Sister Kristen whisper, "Amen." Then she added, "Jaycee, what do you think caused the church to burn down? Is God sending this town, or Father Paul, a message?"

I had no answer for her, so just shook my head. More than ever, I needed to go on a vision quest and search for answers. Until I get things right in my mind and heart, I cannot be of any help to my family or friends.

Chapter 14

The longest journey is the journey inwards. Of
him who has chosen his destiny, who has started
upon his quest for the source of his being.
                                    —Dag Hammarskjold

The world didn't stand still and wait for me, but it disappeared
from my view for a while. Excuses were made, my absence sort of
explained, and the planets went about their orbits. Sun rose and set,
the stars twinkled, prayers floated upward, curses dove downward,
and wolves howled at the moon.

Meanwhile, my so-called recovery was unlike any other I'd
experienced in my fairly short life. I had decided to go on a vision
quest. My parents thought I was staying over at Jaime's and under the
protection of Grandpa Bear—the only person they would trust when
I stayed at a boy's house. And in many ways, they were right. It's true
I had to fudge the truth to both my parents and Grandpa Bear who
was under the impression that my parents were okay with me going
on a vision quest. Of course, they had no clue. This was something
I came to terms with during my second day of the quest. Perhaps,
"come to terms" is an understatement, as I spent the better part of
the morning miserable: hungry, crying, and determined to tell my
parents every lie I'd ever spoken. I find that lying, even tiny white
lies, or keeping secrets from my mom and stepdad is painful. But I
was so mixed up and confused about all that was going on in my life,
I knew I had to do something drastic. That drastic solution was what
I decided to call my vision quest.

It was rather clever, I thought, how I had pulled reeds from the
swamp at the base of a hill, to fashion small cords and tie together

116

random thick branches that, with effort, I was able to break into pieces of about the same length. I then found the tree with a strong branch sticking out about waist high to lean the branches against. I wove bundles of reeds across for protection from the wind and rain. Although, since I had had neither, I didn't have to test my abilities in a real-life situation. Still, with a fire set back a few feet from my lean-to, I could stay warm at night.

When I was finished, I realized that the lean-to, as simple as it was, may have been the proudest I'd felt about anything I had ever made. That first day my smile was wide and my dreams bright. Grandpa Bear told me that Hembleciya meant "crying for a dream." At that time, I was certain it meant crying for praise. In actuality, I would receive none of that from anyone other than myself.

According to Grandpa Bear, I was allowed to carry with me a small bottle of water and no food. The first day was not a problem. I ate like a famished animal a couple of hours before setting off on my quest. By that evening, my stomach was growling, and my lips and mouth were dry. I allowed myself only a quarter of my water. By midday on day two, walking was not as easy and my hunger played with my mind. *"I can sneak off and get some food somewhere. I can eat berries. No one would know."* But, was that as true as I proclaimed to myself? Would my spirit know? Would my spirit understand my pain? Would I see my spirit? And as I retold stories in my head that Grandpa Bear had told me many times before, I gradually calmed myself and did not seek out food, no matter how painful the hunger was by the end of the day.

Sleep was not my friend that night. Cramps struck at my waist, and my stomach was relentless, growling at me. I sipped more water, this time in the middle of the night. Without thinking, I had gulped down the last drop. By morning of day three, I walked as if I had been spinning in circles for an hour. I struggled forward, casually falling from one side to the next, drunk on the world around me. I could feel a change as I made my way toward the swamp. I needed water. A few feet from my lean-to, I realized I no longer had my empty water bottle. I spun to see it near the doused coals from the previous night.

It had to only be ten feet from me—too far. *I must go on to the swamp.* I turned back around and began to walk again.

"Crying for a dream." Looking, searching. I did not understand "crying out" until this moment. I must have been walking for hours trying to reach the swamp. How was it so far away? Only the day before, it had not been so far. I continued on, turning back to see my lean-to as close as it had been an hour ago. Had I even moved? Had I been walking in circles? I was exhausted and parched. My feet were moving by inches until my toes found a rock—hard and steadfast—that sent me falling forward and landing hard on my chest—my face finding much needed water in a mud puddle, although by now I felt nothing. I spit out the mud as it mixed with my tears. "Cry out" meant something to me then, but I didn't have the energy to do so.

Take the path of least resistance. A tall buck stepped up to me, nudging me with its snout. Encouraging me? *Take the path of least resistance.* I tried to clear the fog from my mind, but it wouldn't drift. The buck then, with strength and a powerful leap, strode into a forest, which seemed to open up around the great animal, sucking it in like quicksand. I pushed myself up to follow and found a deer trail.

One step, I gained strength. Two steps, I felt energy. By the third step, I was running along the trail. My arms, body, and face were being lashed with sharp vines and hanging branches, but I felt no pain from any of it. I only felt power, as I seemed to be running with extraordinary speed. Was this my path of least resistance? It was surely a path of freedom and it ended in a ten-foot fall that came upon me without warning. I hit the cliff's edge as if I had intended to jump from it all the while, and landed in the swamp I'd been looking for!

Without a thought to its cleanliness, I took great gulps of the swamp water, wetting my mouth and filling my belly. Even then, in my state of transition and delirium, I wondered if I had lost my spirit. Was I so weak that I would drink this rancid water and allow myself to lose my quest? I stopped and crawled to the shore—soaked. I pulled my clothes off and laid them on a large rock to dry. Then I went back in the water to finish washing the blood and mud from my body as a result of the desperate run through the bushes. Stepping onto the shore again, I found a snake curled on my clothes.

I grabbed a stick and began to prod the creature. It hissed at me and took a snap, barely missing my naked flesh. *The more you poke, the more it will rattle. This creature is dangerous, but you are more powerful.* I don't know where my strength came from, but I threw the stick into the forest and grabbed the snake by its tail and heaved back to throw it. But, as I raised my hand, I realized I was only holding a stick. In the distance, the great buck fled into its welcoming forest.

Suddenly, I was again running and found a rolling meadow where I began playing like a fox pup—rolling and frolicking in a small pack of fox friends. I danced with them on all fours and pawed and wrestled, and in a quick moment, my eyes flashed back to my new friends, seven of them—fist-sized stones, tinted red in color, and lying quietly next to me. Beyond them was a mouse. It was cute with a twitching nose and large listening ears. Then it began running erratically, and I could hear the screech from above as a hawk swooped down and took the mouse in its talons before retreating into the sky. The hawk circled above, and all I could do was cry for the poor little mouse. I wept more than I'd ever wept before. Then I felt the warm snout of the great buck against my shoulder. *It has always been around. You need only open your eyes.*

I did open my eyes, but not as the prophetic buck intended, and it was in time to see the hawk drop the mouse. I jumped up and with great speed, ran toward the falling mouse. As I came underneath the falling creature, my foot struck something hard and sent me tumbling. My hands stretched out as my body struck the ground hard—this time, I felt every bit of the pain. The mouse landed in my hand, looked at me with his big brown eyes, and then scurried off.

I no longer felt the hunger, nor was I parched. I rolled over and looked at the stone I had tripped over, but it was not a stone at all. Rather, it was a buried pipe partially exposed to the world above ground. From it gushed black liquid, which I rubbed my hand against. It was sticky and smooth, a lubricant, and not easy to completely wipe off in the grass, or on my pants.

*****

I was shaking when I woke up. I was lying in my lean-to and warm from still-burning coals. My water bottle was next to me—empty. Jaime was sitting in a camping chair and Grandpa Bear was next to him.

As I struggled to sit up and recover from my dream, Grandpa Bear looked at me and said, "Come. You must tell me what you have just seen."

What I didn't realize was that internally I was being stripped of my false self, the one I had developed, and the one that hides who I truly am. I must first shed those layers before I can find my path. And on day three, I stepped from the small lean-to I had built against a giant ancient walnut tree.

Sadness poured over me as I realized I hadn't had a vision at all. I hadn't cried out. I had only had a dream. A stupid dream.

Chapter 15

AN AWAKENED SPIRIT

Sometimes dreams are wiser than waking.
—Black Elk

Oh, Great Spirit
Whose voice I hear in the winds,
And whose breath gives life to all the world,
hear me, I am small and weak,
I need your strength and wisdom.
Let me walk in beauty and make my eyes ever behold
the red and purple sunset.
Make my hands respect the things you have
made and my ears sharp to hear your voice.
Make me wise so that I may understand the things
you have taught my people.
Let me learn the lessons you have
hidden in every leaf and rock.

I seek strength, not to be greater than my brother,
but to fight my greatest enemy - myself.
Make me always ready to come to you
with clean hands and straight eyes.
So when life fades, as the fading sunset,
my Spirit may come to you without shame."
—A Native American prayer
Translated by Lakota Sioux Chief Yellow Lark, 1887

I don't know how long Jaime and Grandpa Bear had been waiting for me to awaken, but it was long enough for Grandpa Bear to build a shelter—or, as I would soon find out, a sweat lodge.

Upon entering it, I was overcome with billowing clouds steam that blinded me.

"Sit," Grandpa Bear ordered, as he motioned to the open patch of grass on the ground. "Jaime, you must wait outside."

And Jaime did, with no argument.

I'm sure he would have hated being in the sweat lodge. He had always hated sweating on the soccer field, so I don't know how he would have handled being in here where I could hardly breathe.

I sat quietly as Grandpa Bear took a handful of tightly packed and woven reeds, which he then allowed to smoke throughout the room. "I will not give you a pipe," he said, "as is tradition."

"But, why not?" I asked. "I want to learn all the traditions."

He smiled. "Your parents would kill me."

"But, they don't—" I stopped, realizing that I had lied to Grandpa Bear about my parents agreeing with me coming on a vision quest.

"I called them to ask if they would allow you on the Hembleciya. I told them what would happen. They were hesitant at first, but agreed."

"But, they didn't say anything to me. They let me lie to them."

"I am certain you will tell them the truth."

It was as if he'd been on my quest with me. How would he have known what happened to me on my second day?

"Now, tell me about your vision."

"That's the thing, Grandpa Bear. I didn't have a vision. I only had a dream, and I woke up with you and Jaime next to me. I'm so upset with myself. I don't know what I did wrong."

I began to cry and rub my hands along my shorts. *Ugh! This stuff is so gross. Why won't it just come off?*

I looked at my hands—puzzled. What were they covered with . . . ? Was this that stuff from my dream? But, that's impossible. Dreams are not reality. I looked closely at my hands and the syrupy residue. Then again at my shorts, which looked as if they'd been dragged through a mud puddle.

I looked up at Grandpa Bear. "But, it was only a dream. How could I have this stuff on my . . ."

"Now, tell me about your vision."

Smoke enveloped the both of us, and I relayed to Grandpa Bear everything I could remember with extreme clarity. My mind seemed to open and what I could see, I could also taste, smell, and touch. It was as if I were immersed in all elements and levels of the world around me.

When I was done, Grandpa Bear nodded. "I see," was all he said.

I waited, and the two of us sat in silence. Grandpa Bear took out a red pipe and began to smoke. I didn't know what to say. Was he pondering my vision? Was he trying to think of a way to tell me about it? Was something wrong? Why was he saying nothing? So much time had passed with us only sitting in the dark and silence. The glow of burning embers from Grandpa Bear's pipe was the only light remaining, and I realized that dark must have fallen outside. Had we really been in here the entire day?

"Are you going to tell me about my vision? What did I see? What is the meaning?" I blurted, in an intense frustration I'd never known before.

Grandpa Bear took his usual time to respond to my questions, and when he did I couldn't have been more upset.

"It is not time. You are not ready."

Not time? It's hard for me to say I was disgusted with Grandpa Bear, but what else could I think? I went through this whole vision quest. I'd been listening to him for years tell stories of his ancestors and his own personal journey. Yet, when it's my turn it's "not time?"

We had spent the remainder of that day at the campsite. None of us had much to say. Grandpa Bear spent much of his time in the steam shelter. Jaime was gathering wood, berries, and some strange roots I'd never seen before. He then went on to wash and slice the roots, which we then boiled into a steaming tea. For me, I remained in a hammock Grandpa Bear had slung between two trees most of the afternoon watching a different side of Jaime play out before my very eyes.

Jaime had been one of my closest friends for years, yet there was always something about him that seemed out of place, or distant. I'd always assumed there was more to him than what he let on. As I watched him crawl and scuffle on hands and knees at the base of bushes, I couldn't distinguish from one to the other, and I began to realize he did have a life outside of what I knew. He was much more involved in his past than I ever knew. Sure, I wasn't ignorant of his closeness to Grandpa Bear, nor was I ignorant of his interest in his past. But, watching Jaime quickly navigate the underbrush, deftly carve out roots, and then prepare them for . . . for something, I couldn't help but feel a strange sensation in the pit of my stomach—one that I had never felt for Jaime.

I noticed the thin strands of herbs that he was leaving behind at each location where he'd pulled a root, berry, or any of the odd remnants I watched him grab. He looked at me:

"Tobacco," he said. "Grandpa Bear grows it behind the house."

Tobacco?

He went on realizing what I must have been thinking, "Not for smoking. It's left as a gift. A thanks to mother nature for providing me what I need."

I nodded, "I see. And what is it that you need?"

"Grandpa Bear has asked me to prepare a tea for us to enjoy. It will bring back your energy and give you strength. It will also refresh your mind and bring you clarity."

"Oh, well, I could certainly use all that. When can I have some?"

"I can't tell you." He snickered. "I guess when Grandpa Bear is ready to give it to you. He didn't say."

Of course. Grandpa Bear is a man of patience. He did not waste his time in idle chatter. You know, like the kind to tell me what was going on with my own fate. No biggie.

"Here," Jaime said, as he walked over with a cup.

I grabbed the hot cup from his hands and greedily took a deep sip. "Did you make this?"

"Yeah."

"Wow. I didn't know you knew so much about the wilderness, plants, herbs, and all that. How'd you make it? What's in it?"

"Well, this one was a little harder to make than the one I am putting together for later. I boiled water, opened the package, removed tea bag from package, poured boiling water into a cup, and steeped the bag in the water for three minutes. It was a trial of patience."

I punched him in the shoulder.

"It's only chamomile. It will help you relax a bit and ease your nerves."

The tea scorched my tongue and throat, but I didn't care. At that moment, it was the greatest drink I'd ever had. It was a nice change from the gallons of water I think I'd consumed since waking up.

Jaime took the empty cup from me. "I still have more to do. You should rest and try to sleep. It'll pass the time faster than sitting here waiting for Grandpa Bear to finish."

I glanced over at the small tent he'd constructed of leather and furs. Steam poured out the sides and I laughingly pictured him relaxing as if he were at a day spa.

"What's he doing?"

"Talking to his ancestors. He said there was something more to you than he knew. Although, I suspect he knew that all along."

What could that mean? I didn't prompt Jaime any further knowing I wouldn't get anywhere with my questions. The tea was delicious and filled my belly enough for me to feel warm and comfortable moving around. I walked over to the hammock and slid myself into it, covering up with a thin blanket. I'd take Jaime's advice and go to sleep.

*****

There she is. The white squirrel watched Jaycee sleeping in her hammock. He had to sneak away for some time. It's not easy for a squirrel to run . . . well, everything. A small pile of acorns rested in the crook of an ancient oak tree and as the squirrel watched Jaycee, he slowly nibbled on one after another, never seeming to satiate his hunger.

You are coming along fine. I see Grandpa Bear is ready to make his big reveal. But, is it time yet? Not quite. There is so much more you must learn before you are sent on your way. You must be tested. You must show your loyalty. You must make your way over a mountain, which cannot be crossed.

*****

Jaime crossed beneath the tree and looked up. He paused to watch the unusual white squirrel above. He was curious and stared for a few moments. The squirrel stared back. Then as if it knew what it was doing, the squirrel stuck out its tongue at Jaime.

Jaime laughed.

*****

The squirrel thought, *At least Jaycee has some good apostles to follow her on her path. She will need them.*

Chapter 16

AND LO AND BEHOLD, THE EARTH TREMBLED

It takes an earthquake to remind us that we walk
on the crust of an unfinished planet.

—Charles Kuralt

The ground shook harder than I had ever felt it. It was much worse than the other day at home. My hammock swung violently from one side to the other as I could only hang on to avoid falling out. That's when I heard the deafening crack that reverberated and bounced between rocks and hills, like a pinball in a neon arcade.

"What was that?" I screamed out.

I sat up and looked around in every direction, searching for Grandpa Bear and Jaime. Neither was in sight.

The movement of my hammock began to change. It was not only a swinging motion, but also rolling as if I were on a small dingy in the middle of a violent ocean storm. The rocking didn't stop, it only became worse.

The loud crack came again. Then again. The world around me was dizzy and moving too quickly to see anything. My pulse was racing and tears began to stream uncontrollably down my face.

What was happening? Was this another earthquake? I'd never felt one before, and now there were two in less than a week. I scrambled within the confines of the hammock, trying to stabilize it. It completely enveloped me, and I struggled to find even the smallest opening for me to pull it apart and slide free. But, the more I struggled, the more it seemed I became entangled. It was becoming a trap; a straitjacket.

"Jaime!" I screamed as loud as I could. He didn't respond. Where could he be? Where was Grandpa Bear? Was the ground shaking so violently they couldn't even walk? Or, worse, had they di . . . I immediately took the thought from my mind. I couldn't deal with losing either of them.

I frantically tried to find an opening. I needed to get out of the hammock. I heard the loud crack again, and that's when I realized what was happening. The giant trees I had attached the hammock to were cracking. They were slowly breaking. And with me underneath?

How long did these things last? I was trying to think back to Sister Beatrice who taught physical science. I thought earthquakes only lasted seconds. But this felt as if I had been swinging for at least five minutes.

An explosion suddenly ripped through the tree near my head. For a brief moment, everything seemed to stop. Time froze. Complete silence blanketed my world. There was enough time for me to weigh my surroundings. In this brief moment of quiet and stillness, the strangest thing happened.

I trusted Grandpa Bear more than anyone. Maybe even my parents. He was strong, wise, and I always felt he could make any situation better. Yet, as the tree's trunk exploded at its base, and time paused, my eyes sought out Jaime instead of Grandpa Bear. I wanted nothing more than to have Jaime here to save me and console me.

The pause was brief. And when it ended it ended in a fury, throwing my hammock wildly from one side to the next, like a slingshot. I could feel the pressure of the giant falling tree as it came toward me. It had to stand over a hundred feet tall and its trunk was as wide as a car. But, with the shaking, the trunk had snapped like a dry twig, sending splinters flying like shrapnel.

This was the end and I knew it. I could feel the entire force of the tree crushing me like an ant under a shoe. It hadn't quite fallen yet, but I could feel the pressure of it. I could feel . . .

I could feel the tree dying. I could feel its fear and concern. I could hear it say, *"No, not on the little girl. She is so young."*

At that thought, the tree began to tilt in my direction. Its full and voluminous trunk teetered as if balancing on the edge of a skyscraper. The shaking around us—myself and the tree—continued. Although it was not as powerful as before, the shaking was enough to slowly edge the tree's collapse in my direction. I stopped struggling in the hammock. It was to no avail. Instead, I relinquished myself to my fate. I would die here, shortly after my first vision quest. Whatever Jaime had told me Grandpa Bear had seen in me would soon be dissolved as I would be crushed into the soft dirt floor below me. I wondered if Grandpa Bear and Jaime died along with me, would anyone find us? I don't know if my parents even knew where I was.

It was then that I made an important decision. At least for me, I thought it was important. I would watch my fate. I would not succumb to the world around me and close my eyes to it. I would face my fear and accept my fate. If I was going to die in a hammock under a tree during an earthquake, then that is how it would be.

I opened my eyes wide and stared upward. Through a slit in the enveloping hammock, I watched as the giant tree teetered in my direction. I felt the slivers of branches and wood chips snapping off and slamming against my flesh. Still, I refused to close my eyes. I kept them open, forcing myself not to blink.

God, save me! I whispered to myself.

As if he were listening, the hammock fell to the ground in a big thud. I could feel the wind knocked out of me, and I clenched my chest trying to catch my breath.

It took me a moment to realize that the hammock had broken free from the tree.

The tree was falling quicker now than it had before. The trunk must have released itself from the base and I was still under it.

I glanced up to where my hammock had once been strapped to the tree near my feet. The rope was torn as if it had been eaten through. I caught a glimpse of a fluffy white tail flitting around the other side of the tree, and out of sight.

No. It couldn't be? The squirrel couldn't have—

My hammock was suddenly jerked backward and away from the falling tree. I was still trapped inside of the mesh cocoon unable to free myself. I was dragged quickly across the ground as stones and branches dug into my flesh.

*****

The earthquake stopped as quickly as it had begun. Only seconds later, the giant tree fell to Earth, crushing everything underneath it. Had I not been dragged away I would have been one of those things being crushed into sawdust.

Jaime and Grandpa Bear were on either side of me pulling apart the mesh of the hammock in which I had become entangled.

"I didn't think we'd be able to get to you," Jaime said, as his finger deftly removed the debris tied into the hammock's rope, which was likely what had held it shut. "I don't know how you released this thing from the tree, but if you hadn't, we would all be dead now."

I stood up as soon as the hammock opening was released and looked toward the fallen tree. The white squirrel was scrambling away as if it hadn't done anything special at all. But it had. It had saved me. Somehow, that little squirrel had eaten through he hammock strings attached to two trees.

"Umm, yeah. I don't know what happened. The string must have just snapped."

Jaime held the end of the hammock in his hands curiously looking at the break point. "If I didn't know any better I'd say they've been eaten through by some critter."

"Weird," I replied.

Grandpa Bear looked at me and then at the tree. "Yes, 'weird,'" he repeated sarcastically, leaving me with a sneaking suspicion that there was more to what he knew than he was letting on. Even more so than I'd already thought.

A minute later, I was completely free from what had almost been my sarcophagus.

The sun was setting in the west in a brilliant kaleidoscope of orange, red, pink, and purple like I'd never seen before. Despite the light being a little dim, we were able to pack up everything in the camp and head home.

My vision quest had been an adventure greater than anything I'd experienced before—both the quest and what followed. I'd never forget it, and I had a sneaking suspicion that this quest was not over yet. I had learned a lot about the power of the natural world and the power of God. They were intertwined in magical ways that Native Americans had recognized far ahead of later inhabitants of the continent.

Grandpa Bear said nothing as we drove home. Jaime sat next to me in the back. He took my hand and held it the remainder of the way.

I love and admire Grandpa Bear and all that he has taught me and so many others about the old ways. So I wrote a poem inspired by his stories and plan on giving it to him for his seventieth birthday.

New Moon

It was in the moon of the shedding pony,
That we rode out of camp to the river they call
the morning star.
You came with me because,
I knew where I was going,
And you knew that was where you were supposed
to be.
We rode on a horse that was captured on a raid
from our ancient enemy the crow.
She was a spotted war pony with a lancet scar.
Light on her feet with a gait that matched the
wind through the tall grass.
Fear was never known to her.
When we rode you held on to me,
My heart soared and beat with each stride,
As the sacred birds fly without use of their wings.
For one complete moon we lived by the river and
swam with the otters.
And all was as it should be, and as it always was.

We dreamed as in the ancient days before the coming of blue coats and war.
The days slipped into nights.
Each moment was a life and one life was all we ever wanted.
The sun warmed the river and the buffalo traveled their ancient paths.
We knew our life was ending.
We died to each other endlessly,
And time was our only enemy.
I am being called to the hills and my people.
And you to yours.
Memories seared into our hearts and would have to be enough to carry us home to the final resting place where peace would be the world's cloak.

Chapter 17

HOME AGAIN

There is nothing like returning to a place that remains unchanged
to find the ways in which you yourself have altered.
—Nelson Mandela

Driving back into town, things looked familiar to me, yet different. A pall had fallen over the entire town like a cloud of despair.
I said a prayer and vowed right then and there, from the back seat of
Grandpa Bear's big truck, that I would give my life if that's what it
took to save Serenity.

My father and mother had worked far too hard all their lives,
building up their business, to simply give in to whatever evil forces
were at play. I didn't have a plan yet—just a goal. Save Serenity.

It was dark by the time we reached the town center, but the
streetlights were twinkling, welcoming us. Christmas wreaths had
been put up around the lanterns, and there was—as there always
was—a huge evergreen Christmas tree in the plaza square. It was
raised on a platform making it look even bigger, and was decorated
with colorful lights. An angel sat atop the tree, and I could have
sworn she winked at me. Or maybe it was just the light playing tricks.

"Wow, town looks really pretty," I said. "I forgot Christmas is
right around the corner."

"How could you forget, Jaycee?" Grandpa Bear asked, chuck-
ling as he does, which sounds like a burbling brook. "It's your birthday too, right?"

"Yep. I'll be eighteen this year. A grownup."

All I got for that revelation was a grunt. Then, "Go home?"

"Yes, please. I'm dying to see Ghost. And my parents, of course."

A few minutes later, they let me out and helped unload all my camping gear in the driveway. Then they honked the horn and pulled away. As I turned to look at the house, I noticed the white squirrel darting from limb to limb in the big oak tree.

"Hello, Mister Squirrel," I called out.

He squeaked back and seemed to point his little nose at my house.

"Yes, I know," I said. "It looks beautiful, all decorated for Christmas."

Mom and Dad had not waited for me to help decorate, and I was a bit disappointed by that. Before I could feel sorry for myself, the front door opened, and Mom and Dad came running out. Hugs all around.

"Welcome home, honey. We didn't expect you until tomorrow," Mom said, smelling like gingerbread.

"Apparently," I chastised them. "You didn't even wait for me . . ."

"Jaycee, things have been so depressing, we just wanted to cheer ourselves up." Dad rubbed his tummy. "Mom has been baking non-stop, feeding our feelings, she calls it." He laughed.

They helped me haul my stuff inside, and I took a shower and put on my jammies. Then, with a cup of hot chocolate, overflowing with tiny marshmallows, and a plate of cookies, I sat cross-legged on the floor under the ten-foot tall Christmas tree in our living room bay window.

For at least those few minutes, all was right with the world. The house smelled like cinnamon and ginger; Dad even had an old Bing Crosby album of carols playing in the background. It was as though I had gone from a very disturbing vision quest to some after-school Christmas special on TV.

Then the doorbell rang.

I answered it and let the whole gang in. Maggie and all the rest of our friends were there and said they were happy to see me home and safe. We did our "group hug" thing, and Mom brought us a plate of cookies. Then we got down to business.

"Jaycee," Maggie said, "something very bad is going on in this town. We are the next generation. We need to do something."

"Well, Mags, look at you being all full of civic responsibility," I said, teasing her. "Who knew you were so . . ."

She punched me in the arm. "Hey, I'm a citizen. I care."

Suddenly, everyone was talking at once, about the church being burned, how devastated Father Paul was about losing all his precious collections that could never be replaced, how Whalemart was coming to town and would put all their parents (and mine) out of work and into bankruptcy, how Sister Kristen didn't know what she was going to do with all her homeless animals, and how the mayor had given a press conference saying that the city would be better off with a big box chain store in town that would draw new residents and increase the tax base. Blah, blah, blah . . .

"What are we going to do, Jaycee?"

They all stared at me like I had answers.

"Guys, right this minute, I have no idea. But I do know that the answers will come. I want you all to go home and pray about it. Meditate. Brainstorm. The universe will give us the solutions. Let's meet right back here in two days and figure out a plan of action!"

It was December 22.

My birthday party would also be a meeting and a chance for our group to save our little town.

Chapter 18

THE END IS JUST THE BEGINNING

We shall not cease from exploration, and the end
of all our exploring will be to arrive where we
started and know the place for the first time.

—T. S. Eliot

I awoke on the twenty-third feeling refreshed and full of hope. Admittedly, things didn't look good for our town, but I had tremendous hope and optimism.

My mom's voice sang out from the kitchen—cooking is her therapy, "Jaycee, you up, honey? Breakfast is ready!"

It smelled like a Denny's restaurant, with sausage, bacon, pancakes, warm syrup, cinnamon rolls, and coffee. Of course, hot chocolate simmered in a copper pot. She set one down in front of me with a candy cane to stir it.

"Merry Christmas, Mom," I said, kissing her on the cheek.

"Well, honey, it may not be our happiest, but we will do our best. Sales have been good at the store. I think people are just beginning to appreciate all the things your father does. They are showing their loyalty. It's nice to see."

I sipped the hot cocoa and let it scald my throat. "It will all be okay, Mom. Not sure how, but it will."

I gave her my best Jaycee brand of smile, which she always said I should patent.

After packing on a few thousand carbs and enough sugar to power a windmill, I set out to see Father Paul. He was staying in a construction trailer on the church grounds, and they had placed another trailer in an L-shape to use as a sanctuary. The Catholic Church was not about to let the town go without a place to worship (and donate) during the all-important Christmas holiday season. Fire or no fire, church business went on.

Father Paul answered the door wearing corduroy slacks and a holiday sweater, looking pretty chipper for someone who had lost his most prized possessions. He was quick to set me straight, "Jaycee, come in. I was just having some tea. Care for a cup?"

"No, thanks, Father," I answered, ready to gag at the thought of putting one more morsel in my belly. "My mom is in holiday over-drive and cooking like the world's going to end soon and everybody is hungry."

He laughed. "During trying times, we need to remember the words of my namesake, Saint Paul, who said, 'I can do all things through Christ who strengthens me. For the wisdom of this world is foolishness with God. If there is a natural body, there is also a spiritual body.' Soon, we will have a new sanctuary, I will have a new home, and in the meantime, I am grateful to have this wonderful shelter that is heated and even comes equipped with cable TV!"

"Wow," I said. "Cable TV, huh?"

We had a good laugh, both of us thinking about his beautiful artifacts and priceless collections, gone forever. I didn't dare bring that up. But I did have to ask, "So, Father, have you heard any news about what caused the fire?"

"The police tell me that it was definitely arson, although I can't for the life of me fathom who would want to burn down a church. I'm inclined to think it was something to do with the earthquakes. Or perhaps a message to me."

"Message?" *Hmmm, this is interesting. Has the good father been a bad boy?*

"I'm like any mortal man, Jaycee. The robes I wear are the mantle of God, not my own. I am a sinner, yes, I am. I just hope I haven't sinned to the degree that such a drastic message was required to set me straight."

"I'm sure that's not the case," I said, trying to ease his obvious misery. "You are a good man. But those collections . . ." *Oops, me and my big mouth.*

"Yes, my beautiful coins and other lovelies. They are gone, to be sure. But losing them has been a blessing in disguise."

His smile was small and tight, weaker than I'd ever seen, as he is normally given to big and dramatic gestures. He laughs big, cries big, and usually has a big smile, especially at the holidays. And near my birthday. But tonight, he looked like a kid who's been caught with his hand in the cookie jar.

"How so, Father? How is losing everything a so-called blessing?"

"Well, Jaycee, I had gotten too comfortable, too complacent with all my stuff and things. Probably a bit lazy as well. This fire, no matter who or what started it, was a wakeup call. I had to prepare an inventory for the fire marshal and the insurance claims adjuster. The list was astonishing. And the value, you were right, Jaycee. That money could have helped a lot of people. I will not make that mistake again."

Hmmm. I was right? Wow. But I said, "Father, if you're talking about my questioning why the church is so wealthy . . ."

"Yes, that's exactly what I'm talking about. Not that the Vatican is wrong, but that we must always think about long term good and not amass wealth for the sake of it. Security is one thing. Greed is another."

"So, who do you think started the fire?"

"I think it all has to do with the arrival of the big Whalemart Store. It's too coincidental. I haven't put everything together in my mind yet, but I think it's all connected."

"I agree," I said, silently ashamed that I had thought Father Paul might be behind the greedy land grab. "Would it be wrong to say I think the mayor is on the take?"

Father Paul poured himself another cup of tea and stood by the window, holding the curtain aside. "It's starting to snow," he said.

"God's gift to winter. A blanket of white covers everything. Cracked sidewalks, trash cans, everything except our sins."

He turned from the window and finally addressed my question. "Why would you think such a thing, Jaycee?"

"I saw him pocket an envelope at the ball field. Some strange men gave it to him. He looked happy and shook their hands like a deal had been made. Now, all the land in town is either being bought up outright by Whalemart or being taken by imminent domain. It looks sketchy, right?"

"I must say, my dear, that it does look suspicious, but we must not jump to conclusions. That envelope could have contained anything. But I agree that this requires further investigation."

"Maybe me and my posse can do some digging," I said, only half serious.

What could a bunch of teenagers do?

"Good idea. Who would suspect you and your friends, Jaycee? But be careful. Don't get in over your head." He paused. "What did you learn on your so-called vision quest?"

I couldn't help but think he sounded a bit jealous, or petulant, like I was seeking wisdom from some place other than the church, which I was. But I didn't think he would be upset by it. Seeking wisdom is a good thing, right?

"I learned a lot about myself, and a lot about the power of our natural world, Father. It taught me that God can be found in many places and takes many forms. There's this adorable little white squirrel."

"A squirrel, child? What does that have to do with anything?"

"Never mind. I was thinking out loud which is never good with me."

I laughed at myself, and he joined along.

"Well, tomorrow is Christmas Eve and your birthday too. Do you have big plans?"

"I do. And I have a big, big wish for my birthday gift. I'm hoping for a new car. If I'm going to college next fall, I will need a mode of transportation. But that isn't likely since Dad is so worried about losing his store. It's just all a big confusing mess!"

"God's will be done. Whatever is meant to be will be, Jaycee. It's all in His hands."

"But we can still wish, Father!" I refused to let him bring me down. God's will or not, I need transportation. What I didn't bring up, because I'm not ready to share it, is that my path may not be college at all.

Chapter 19

BIRTHDAY

Then the Grinch thought of something he hadn't before!
What if Christmas, he thought, doesn't come from a store.
What if Christmas . . . perhaps . . . means a little bit more!
—Dr. Seuss, How the Grinch Stole Christmas!

December 24 dawned cold with clear icy-blue skies. No snow in the forecast, but I was hopeful, as it always seems more special with a fresh blanket of snow.

Knock knock knock. "Come in," I sang out, ready to receive my traditional birthday breakfast of Cheetos, Twinkies, and canned soda. Mom and Dad have been doing that every year to remind me that I was born in a roadside rest area between two vending machines. It's their way of "keeping me humble" they say, although why they worry about my being humble is a mystery. What do I have to be conceited about? Certainly not my mediocre soccer skills. Just ask Maggie. She will tell you I often suck.

Ghost was not happy about being shushed off the bed, but he jumped down anyway, mainly because I shoved him. He's such a big lug.

"Happy birthday to you," they came in singing, each carrying a platter of junk food snacks.

"Aw, thanks, you guys," I said, hugging both my parents tightly. I love them so, so much. "I am eighteen today. Do I have to move out?"

They both laughed. "Don't even think about it, Jaycee," my dad said.

"Certainly not," my mom echoed the sentiment. "Not until you are married. And even then . . ."

"What if I become a nun, Mom? Would that be okay with you? No chance for grandkids . . ."

"We are behind you, honey, whatever you decide. But I think that business about priests and nuns not marrying is ridiculous and old-fashioned. Maybe one day soon it will change. This new Pope . . ."

"I agree, Mom," I said. "But I was just testing you. I'm not nun material, I'm afraid. I'm far too stubborn and too nosy to make a good sister."

"Jaycee, your heart is as big as the ocean. You would make an excellent servant of the Lord, no matter what path you choose. But I am hoping for college, you know that," Dad said.

After crumbling some Cheetos over scrambled eggs—my healthy concession to Mom's desire for me to eat something substantial for breakfast—I texted everyone to meet me at Sister Kristen's animal shelter. I knew she would be there with the lights and heat on, Christmas Eve or not.

Soon, my friends and I, including Maggie, were gathered in the tiny reception area where people brought animals in or adopted them. It was shabby but warm, and I love the posters of cute kittens and puppies plastered on every wall.

"Okay, gang, here's the deal," I began. "Sorry for changing our plans, but things are even more serious than I'd thought. There is something strange going on in this town, and it's going to be up to us to figure it out. Otherwise, all of our parents will be unemployed, failed business owners, or bankrupt."

Heads nodded, and I noticed that Letty was wide-eyed, and Madison looked like she'd been crying. I definitely had everyone's attention. I saw movement out of the corner of my eye and realized it was Ghost, circling and trying to get comfortable on the grungy sofa. I had brought him with me to make sure he got an outing. He always seems happiest when we're together, which is pretty much always. He even sleeps on the foot of my bed, which means there's hardly any room for me.

Madison said, "What can we do to help, Jaycee? Happy birthday, by the way."

"Thanks, Maddy. You're all coming to my house later for my party, right?"

All heads nodded. "Awesome. And you will all be dead meat if you bring any gifts. But donations to the church's building fund— see Father Paul for details—will be welcome."

More head bobbing and a few smiles. Just then, Ghost scared the crud out of us with a loud bark. He jumped up and put his nose against the window. Lo and behold, as we turned to see what he was barking at, that darned adorable white squirrel was perched on the window sill, wiggling its nose at us.

"Ghost, sit down," I yelled at him. "You scared us!"

What is the deal with that squirrel?

"Okay," I said, drawing everyone's attention back to me and the subject at hand. "Does anyone know who, how, or why the church was set on fire? I'm hearing that it might have been faulty wiring."

Madison said, "My mom says she heard at work in the City Hall that the sheriff and the fire chief both think it was some kind of natural causes. Like lightning. But nobody saw any lightning, so . . ."

"Does anyone think it's related to Whalemart, or is it just a coincidence?" I asked.

Blank stares. No one seemed to have a clue.

"Okay, let's put that aside for now, but keep your ears open. Father Paul is very upset about it, but he's determined to rebuild. I think he has a much more modest chapel in mind, and maybe just an apartment for him to live in. Definitely a community hall space and kitchen for events. We can get to work after the holidays and raise money. Everyone in?"

Murmurs of yes, sure, and you got this were welcome sounds to my ears. My friends are as loyal as they come.

"Okay, now to the looming thoughts of Whalemart coming to town. What do we think about that?"

Maggie, who had been quiet up until now, finally stood up to say her peace. "Look, guys, I know you all think poorly of my parents. Lord knows I've had my issues with them. And they do have their faults. But my dad loves this town and wouldn't do anything to hurt it or the people who live here."

Letty said, "Maggie, no one is blaming your parents."

"I know everyone thinks because Devlin Carless is president of the bank, and my dad is the chairman of the bank's board of directors, that they are evil. But they're not . . ."

I jumped in with, "Of course Mr. Carless and your parents . . . your dad . . . are not evil, Mags. No one thinks that."

"I hope not," Maggie said, for once seeming genuinely interested in a topic beyond boys, her latest new outfit, or even her current condition, which only I knew about.

Johnny Carless, who had also been quiet, said, "My dad is not a mean man, Jaycee."

"Okay, Johnny. We know. But have you heard him talk about Whalemart?"

"No, Jaycee. He whispers when he is on the telephone, so I cannot hear him, Jaycee."

"Okay, guys. Here's what we know. Whalemart is buying up land like it's going out of style. Apparently, they want to build a big store here. If they do, it will put all the small mom-and-pop-owned stores out of business."

Johnny raised his hand. "Jaycee, who are mom and pop?"

I sighed, trying to stay patient. "It's an expression, Johnny. Anyway, we need to find out who owns the land the strip mall is on. Maybe we could somehow convince them not to sell to Whalemart."

Everyone seemed to think that was a good idea.

Maggie said, "But, Jaycee, it's Christmas. City hall offices are closed. Why don't we plan to get back together on January 3 or so, and in the meantime, everyone should keep ears and eyes open for clues. Especially you, Johnny. You need to listen in and see what your dad knows and who he's talking to. I'll do the same thing. We can figure this out!"

We got into a circle, piled our hands on top of each other, and let out a loud *whoop*!

"Okay, meeting adjourned," I said. "Next stop, my birthday party! Cheetos and Fritos for everyone!"

*****

All my friends left to go about their Christmas Eve duties—Father Paul was holding a carol singing event and some of them had signed up to go—so I stayed behind to help Sister Kristen feed and clean cages. She still hadn't been able to find homes for all of them. Her blue eyes were sparkling feverishly, and her smile seemed forced, but she was hanging in there and hopeful.

"Do you really think you and your friends can keep this land from being sold, Jaycee?"

"I think we can, Sister. Hope springs eternal. We have youth and energy on our side, even if we don't have a lot of business and real estate know-how. Sometimes, passion is more valuable than experience."

She smiled, but I think she was skeptical. For a nun, Sister Kristen seems to have very little faith—that's something I hope I can help her overcome soon.

*****

By the time I got home, the tree lights were sparkling, Father Paul was sitting in my dad's overstuffed recliner chair with a mug of tea, and the house smelled like mulled cider. The aroma of Christmas was in the air: cinnamon, nutmeg, cardamom, eggnog, and chocolate. Christmas carols were playing softly, coming from a little radio my dad had had for decades, and both my parents had on their ridiculous matching holiday sweaters.

"Jaycee," my mom said sternly, "go up and put on your sweater too. You know it's our tradition. We have to get a picture by the tree."

I did as I was told, Ghost bouncing right on my heels. Mom had my sweater laid out on my bed along with a beautiful card. The poem she wrote made me cry, and I will not share it with you. It's too personal. But here's a snippet of poetry from my wonderful mom:

Once upon a rainy night
A skyward light flashed black to bright.
Our baby girl was born to all,
A child who talked before she could crawl.
Eighteen years of heart and soul,
Teenage angst that takes a toll.

*****

I wiped away the tears—my mom's sweet poems always make me weepy and silly—and headed back downstairs to find no one. Not a soul in sight. Ghost looked at me as though he was confused too. The cider bubbled on the stove, the tree sparkled, the carols played, all to an empty house.

"Hey, where is everybody?" I yelled.

Then, I heard the honk of a car horn. *What? Who would be here on Christmas Eve?*

I ran outside and there was everyone—my mom, Dad, and all my friends forming a barricade on the sidewalk. As I walked out the door, they split apart and revealed the old blue van that had been covered and in the shed for eighteen years. Last time I had looked at it, the tires were flat, and it looked sad and abandoned—the old Chevy van—the one Mom and Dad had been driving on that rainy night when I was born. Soon after, so the story goes, they had retired the van, gotten a new more family-appropriate sedan, and forgotten about it.

And now the van was back, all shiny and bright, new tires, and a modern license plate. What the heck?

Dad walked up to me and handed me a key. "The old van is now yours, Jaycee. It's been completely overhauled and should be safe for you to drive." He smiled proudly. "Happy birthday, daughter dear!"

"It's mine?" I was beyond excited.

Mom said, "Yes, honey, it's all yours. We even had the title changed to your name. Wherever the highway of life takes you, it will carry you safely, as it carried us to that roadside rest area eighteen years ago. But you better be careful!"

I was so happy. What a great birthday. "Can we take it for a spin?"

I didn't even wait for an answer. I ran over, jumped in the driver's seat, and Maggie and all my friends piled inside. We didn't go far, just around the block, but it was so much fun. What a great birthday. What a great Christmas Eve.

And then we saw it. Just as I pulled back into the driveway, a huge bright light flashed across the sky, illuminating the darkness. Ghost barked. The squirrel bounced on the tree limb and created a snow shower on our heads. And I thought, *Light will always split the darkness. Hope defies evil. And our town will be all right.*

Later that evening when the town and all in Serenity were sleeping I reached for my poem journal and wrote this. It seems to flow from my pen as if channeled and I knew then that my purpose here was just beginning to unfold.

The Second Time Around

No one saw me coming.
No one shows their pain.
Never thought i would find you here.
Lost with so much left to gain.
Some how my message got missed.
My words got washed away as you rode the gold
and silver train.
Why do you hurt each other?
Why do you play these earthly games?
The lights are going dim.
The heavens clouded by some much prejudicial
shame.
The second time around my arms are wide open.
I want to bring you all home with me the seeing
and the blind.
Compassion and love were the simple truths i
meant to teach and leave behind.
Give more then you take is simply all i meant to say.
No one saw me coming.
Some how you lost your way.
The second time around my arms are wide open.
I want to bring you all home with me.
The seeing and the blind.

Most think god could only wear a kings crown
and with a male scepter rule the earthly plane.
Some how, some way, men and women forgot,
both were born from gods vein.
Compassion and love were the simple truths, the
teaching i left behind.
The second time around my arms are wide open.
I want to bring you all home with me this time
the seeing and the blind.

About the Author

I have lived in the St. Paul, Minnesota area my whole life. My schooling consisted of twelve years of private Catholic education, four years of which was in an all-male military high school. As a young man, I worked in the Boundary Waters Canoe Area, and that's where my love of nature was nurtured. Later in life, I had the privilege to meet an elder of a local Native American community. His name was Bear, and he taught me some of the ancient traditions of his tribe. I believe we should show respect for all forms of life – both human and animal – with whom we share this planet.

I hope you enjoy my tale.